DANGEROUS HEARTS

TAKEBACK
BOOK 6

RILEY EDWARDS

BE A REBEL
Riley Edwards Romance

DANGEROUS HEARTS
TAKEBACK book 6

Cover design: Lori Jackson Designs

Written by: Riley Edwards

Published by: Riley Edwards/Rebels Romance

Edited by: Kendall Black

Proofreader: Julie Deaton

Proofreader: Rylee Smith

Book Name: Dangerous Hearts

Paperback ISBN: 978-1-951567-54-5

First edition: October 31, 2023

To my family - my team — my tribe.
This is for you.

CONTENTS

CHAPTER ONE

Jane Morgan.

There she was.

Only she was no longer Jane Morgan, she was now Calypso Gardner. Before that she'd been Harley Jenkins. And before that, she was Corinne Lawrence—the name she'd been given at birth.

The woman had not only changed her name, but she'd bleached her hair blonde and cut it to her shoulders. The length suited her, but her natural dark hair looked better against her pale complexion.

Either way, the woman was a knockout—but dark as she was fucking gorgeous.

A knockout sitting on a stool at a bar alone.

That made my play a no-brainer.

I made my way across the crowded tiki lounge and sat on the stool right next to hers even though there were half a dozen empties that wouldn't put me in her space.

Her head turned, presumably to see who'd sat next to her.

I opened my mouth to say something but immediately closed it.

Spectacular green eyes full of fear locked with mine. Jane's body swung back, and her lips parted. Lips that were undoubtedly shiny from gloss, but that would look better if they were wet from my kiss. Her now-tanned-from-the-Hawaiian-sun cheeks colored pink, taking her beauty from gorgeous to leaving a man speechless.

This woman was the sister of a man I despised.

A piece of shit I was going to help put in jail.

She was also the woman who was going to help me do just that.

That was, if I didn't drown in those extraordinary eyes first.

Her shoulders slumped and she whispered, "You found me."

Indeed I had.

After months of looking.

"You know who I am?" I asked.

"Yes, Mr. Wright, I know who you are."

I took in her stylish sundress, the dangling earrings, the thin silver chain around her neck, all the way down to her sandaled feet. Nothing about her said biker bitch; not the way she dressed, not her understated makeup, not her posture, not the way she spoke. Yet her brother, Zeus, was the president of the Horsemen MC.

Jane came out of her slump, squared her shoulders, and asked, "Why are you here?"

"Why am I here?" I repeated.

"Yes, Mr. Wright, that's what I asked."

I could get down with her calling me Mr. Wright in her sweet, prim, sexy voice while I was balls deep inside of her and she was panting my name. But right then when it was laced with condescension it pissed me off.

"Did you forget?" I returned.

"Forget what?"

"You called us," I reminded her.

A few months back, Jane Morgan had called the Takeback office asking to speak to my boss, Wilson McCray. We'd been in the middle of a situation, therefore unable to take the call. By the time Wilson had returned Jane's call, her number was disconnected. I'd gone by her place to find it still fully furnished, but she was nowhere to be found. A quick check showed she hadn't used her credit cards or bank account since she'd made the call. And with her brother being who he was, that sent up red flags.

"I don't understand how a phone call leads to you flying across the Pacific to track me down."

"You don't?"

Before Jane could answer, the bartender stopped in front of us and tipped his chin.

"Nothing for me," I told him before he could ask for my drink order. I glanced at Jane's empty glass. "Do you need a refill?"

"No, thank you. Just the check, please."

I watched as she lifted a small purse off of her lap, unzipped the clutch, and pulled out a credit card.

I snatched the card before she could hand it to the bartender and checked the name.

Calypso Gardner.

New identity. New credit card. New bank account in her fake name. That didn't come cheap, at least not good documentation that would hold up under heavy scrutiny. Which meant, she'd paid a fortune, something she couldn't have afforded according to Jane Morgan's bank accounts.

"Hey," she snapped.

"Zeus pay for that?" I asked and placed the card on the bar.

The woman flinched, actually flinched at the mention of her brother.

What she didn't do was answer.

"Why are you here?" She went back to her earlier question.

I waited for the bartender to place Jane's bill in front of her, waited even longer while she looked it over, then pushed her card toward the man.

As soon as he walked away I educated her on something I'd assume she was already well-versed in but it seemed she wanted to play dumb.

"When women connected to your brother go missing, we pay attention. When that woman contacted us right before she goes missing, we not only take notice, we go looking for her. And we take notice because your brother is a morally bankrupt, piece of shit who treats women like property that can be rented out or sold."

That got me another flinch.

What the fuck?

She had to know what her brother was into or at the bare minimum what he was capable of.

When she didn't say anything I prompted, "Does that answer your question?"

"Yes," she whispered.

"Now are you going to explain why you called then disappeared?"

"I'd rather not."

That wasn't the response I was looking for but it was at least honest.

The bartender was back, sliding her fake-name credit card and receipt in front of her. She took her time spelling out Calypso Gardner in pretty, scrolling letters and I wondered if that was to buy her time or if she was concentrating on remembering not to sign Jane Morgan—which was not the name she was born with but the name she'd used the longest.

Why so many name changes?

Who was she hiding from?

I waited for her to put her card back into the ridiculously

small purse before I pushed for an answer knowing my next move wouldn't win me any favors.

"You know protecting him makes you just as guilty as he is."

"Protecting who?"

I felt my jaw clench.

"Zeus," I bit out.

"I'm not protecting Trevor. I have nothing to do with his business."

I didn't believe that.

"When you called, you told Mia that Zeus told you to call us."

"I did."

Christ, this was like pulling teeth. If I didn't know any better, I'd think the woman worked in law but I knew she'd been an office manager for a fence company for the last few years.

"Why did he tell you to call us?"

"He thought Takeback would help me but after I made the call, I thought about it, and realized there was no way Wilson would help the sister of the man who he's trying to put down."

Interesting.

"So you know Takeback's actively investigating your brother but you're not involved in his business."

Jane's eyes went from alert and darting around the mostly empty bar area to narrowed on me in a flash.

"That's exactly what I'm saying. You can't live in Coeur d'Alene and not know Wilson McCray has made it his personal mission to dismantle the Horsemen and with that take down my brother."

That might be true but I wasn't buying it.

"Yet he thought a man who thinks he's a piece of shit would help his sister. Why's that?"

"Because Trevor thinks that Wilson's a good man who

would help a woman whose father has promised her as payment, despite the issues between them," she hissed, and I tucked away that information.

Now it was my turn to flinch.

"What the fuck?" I raged. "Your father promised you as payment? Not that it matters but what the hell are you supposed to be payment for?"

"You're right, it doesn't matter. None of it does. I'm here and he hasn't found me yet so it's all good."

That was naïve as shit. If I could find her, someone else could as well.

"Hate to break it you, Jane, but your man in Oregon gave you up and all it cost me was five grand."

Her lips parted and brows pinched.

"Asshole," she breathed.

She got that right.

"So, it matters—all of it. And as much as it pains me—and I mean my gut is turning as I say this—but your brother's right. Wilson is a good man, and if you'd waited a day for him to call you back you could've saved yourself a fuckton of cash on that new identity that's now worthless and we would've gotten you someplace safe."

Her gaze slid away and her posture slumped back to defeated.

"Actually, *nothing* matters anymore," she rasped and stood. "This was always going to end this way."

Everything about Jane Morgan screamed beaten down and dejected. She was a complex riddle; nothing about her made sense. What was worse, everything about the woman called to me—the sister of a man I was going to help put in prison.

CHAPTER TWO

I wasn't sure who I hated more, my father or my brother. No, that wasn't true, I hated my father more but only because I remembered when my brother wasn't the ruthless motorcycle club president. Though over the years it had become harder and harder to remember Trevor when he was my loving brother and protector. Now, he was damn near unrecognizable, but I saw a glimpse of him return when I went to his clubhouse to tell him about our father's threats. For a split second he reverted back to the big brother I loved. But, again, that had only lasted a second then he went back to being Zeus.

Ugh.

I hated that name.

Trevor was not the king of the gods. He was a broken boy who'd grown up to be a broken man who instead of seeking help turned into our father—a criminal, an abuser, a despicable human who valued nothing.

There had been times when I wondered if Trevor was so far gone he'd turn on me.

"Where are you going?" Davis asked from behind me.

Another reason to hate Trevor—Davis Wright.

Of all the men who worked for Takeback it had to be Davis who came looking for me. If the men thought they were flying under the radar they were wrong. As soon as the eight men had hit Idaho they were the topic of gossip. Eight hot newcomers who were all built like fitness models turned heads, even in a town such as Coeur d'Alene where there was no shortage of good-looking men.

So, I'd noticed all eight. I'd seen them at Smutties hanging out and at the bakery two doors down. Not that I'd be welcomed into either of those places again now that my secret was out and they all knew I was Zeus's—*insert gagging*—little sister. But it was Davis Wright who'd captured my attention with his brown hair, blue eyes, and broad shoulders. I'd never seen him clean shaven, just like now he always had what looked like a few days' worth of stubble. Not a full beard, not a five o'clock shadow, but just enough facial hair to make him look rugged and manly instead of like Grizzly Adams.

"Jane," he snapped when I kept walking.

"Calypso," I corrected.

I was Calypso Gardner now. Not that I'd be her for long seeing as my guy in Oregon had given me up. Which meant if Davis found me, so could my father.

"To pack," I told him without looking back.

Pack and go where?

Back to Idaho?

My feet hadn't even hit the hot sand when Davis's hand wrapped around my bicep and spun me around.

"Where are you going?" he asked again.

"I told you, to pack."

He shook his head and followed up the gesture with the same question, "Where are you going?"

"I don't know, somewhere not here."

"Tell me about your father."

Oh, no. Hell, no. I'd stupidly listened to my brother once

and called Wilson for help. I'd known better than to ask Trevor's mortal enemy for anything, yet I'd been so freaked out I'd made the call. Now I had Davis poking around in family business.

Family business that would give him and Takeback more ammunition to use against my brother. Not that I made it a habit of covering for Trevor or his club. But I didn't want any part of Takeback's dealings with the Horsemen. I'd done everything I could to keep my distance and my connection to Trevor a secret. And Trevor had kept my existence a secret from his club. No one knew he had a sister. Heck, I wasn't even sure if anyone in the club knew who our father was.

"I don't want to talk about my father."

That was the understatement of the century.

There were stretches of time when I could forget I had a father, a brother, or a mother for that matter and live the fake life I had created for myself. Part of that life was pretending I'd been born to regular, nice, loving parents.

"So let me get this straight," Davis spat. "You'd rather your father use you as payment than explain to me what's going on and let me help you."

Damn, I can't believe I let that slip.

And when he put it like that, it made me sound like I was a twit.

"No, I don't want my father to use me as payment," I returned with the same sarcasm. "I don't even want to remember I have a father. I want to go about my life, living in my bubble. I don't want Trevor's help—"

"That's the first smart thing you've said," he cut me off.

Asshole.

"I see you think I'm stupid, Mr. Wright, but I assure you I'm not. I know who my brother is."

"Yet, you waltz your ass into his clubhouse, in your tight skirt and high heels, and when you did that you drew attention. A lot of attention, the kind a smart woman wouldn't want."

I didn't need to be reminded of my foolish moment of weakness. No, it wasn't weakness, it was desperation. But in my defense, what's a woman to do when her father sends one of his lackeys to retrieve her? The only place I could go was the Horsemen compound. The one place my father's minion would never step foot in.

"Because the better option would've been to allow myself to be taken back to my father. Right, I see. How stupid of me. I should've just gone back to Montana and offered myself up for a life of misery."

"Who's your father?"

That was easy.

"The devil."

Davis did a slow blink and dropped his hand from my arm.

"Name," he demanded.

"Satan."

I could see the frustration mounting in Davis's expression and for some reason that frustration gave me a momentary thrill. Good, I was glad he felt this exchange was just as irritating as I did.

"Jane—"

"My father's name is Satan," I cut in.

"Come again?"

"Satan," I said slowly. "His name is Satan and I assure you it fits. The man is the devil. There's a reason Trevor is the way he is and it's because of our father."

That was another understatement.

Trevor wasn't who he was because of our father. He was who he was because our father had beaten Trevor into the man he'd become.

The son of a one-percenter.

The abused had become the abuser.

And that was not an excuse. Trevor knew right from wrong, or he had when we were younger. Then the 'thing' happened and a switch flipped in my brother and he turned into a monster.

"I take it your father is a biker," Davis rightly deduced.

"If by biker you mean a scumbag, then yes. Though, just to say, not all bikers are bad people."

"Why won't you tell me his name? You have to know all it would take is one call to the office and I'd have all the information I need."

I didn't know for certain what Davis could or couldn't get by calling the office. Though I could guess, seeing as he was standing in front of me after tracking me all the way to Hawaii.

There had been a time in my life when the thought of someone finding out who my father was would've given me an anxiety attack. I'd long since moved past that, and hid my real identity as a safety precaution. Though that didn't stop me from making up flowery stories about my childhood to make myself feel better.

"By all means, waste your time and call your office. You knowing who my father is changes nothing."

"Why the fuck are you being so stubborn about this?"

"Why the fuck won't you mind your business and drop it?"

Davis's head tipped to the side, a deep scowl etched into his brow, and his eyes narrowed.

The look was menacing, but his posture was what had my attention—he looked like he was on the verge of snapping.

"What's the real reason you don't want to tell me?"

"The real reason?"

"Yeah, the reason." Davis stepped closer and dipped his chin. "What are you afraid I'll find, Jane? What's your involvement in your father's club?"

Yup. The man was an asshole. Which was typical—most hot guys were total pricks.

Two can play this game.

On an inhale I pushed my shoulders back and stood my ground. I'd been around dangerous men my whole life. Men that would have no problem lashing out at a woman and striking her. Davis didn't seem the type to hit a woman, especially in public but I had long ago stopped cowering.

"I see you've already made up your mind about me," I started and shrugged. "You're not the first judgmental asshole I've come across and you won't be the last."

With that, I walked away from Davis Wright for the second time that day.

This time he didn't follow.

I made it to my room, ignored the hurt, and started to pack.

CHAPTER THREE

I had been called a lot of names in my life, however, judgmental had never been one of them.

I stood outside in the warm Hawaiian sun and watched Jane as she entered the hotel. I stood there longer, giving her time to catch an elevator up to our floor. By the time I was back in my room I was no less perplexed but I was smiling as I pulled my lockpicking kit from my bag and tossed it on the dresser.

First things first.

I needed information.

I'd start with my teammate, Rhode. He'd have no trouble running a search on Jane's father. Once I had the basics I'd have Wilson get in contact with Shepherd Drexel, a hacker we frequently used and have him dig up the dirt on Jane's father.

The phone rang twice before Rhode answered, "How's Hawaii?"

"Frustrating. I need you to find Jane's father. She mentioned Montana, so I'd start there. The only other info I got out of her was he's a biker and goes by the club name, Satan."

"Satan?" Rhode spat.

"Yup. Jane called him the devil and implied he was on the level of Zeus."

"She give you anything else?"

"Just that she called at Zeus's suggestion because her father's planning on using her as payment."

I'd known Rhode Daley a long time—I didn't need to see the man to know he was now vibrating with the same anger I'd felt when Jane had slipped up and told me what she was running from. And I knew it was a slip-up; the crazy woman would rather go on the run by herself than accept our help.

"The fuck?" Rhode seethed. "Payment?"

"That's what she said."

"Not that it fucking matters but did she tell you what she's payment for?"

Yep, same response I'd had.

"She's not being very forthright. As in, she's not talking at all."

I could hear Rhode angrily tapping on his keyboard, but it was the whistled exhale that made my jaw tighten.

"What'd you find?" I asked.

"Apple didn't even fall off the tree with these two," Rhode started. "Everything from armed robbery to shoplifting."

"Name," I growled. Jesus, was this guy's name top secret?

"Carl Lawrence. Sixty-five. He's done three stints in jail. One for grand theft auto, did nine months—released early for good behavior and inmate overpopulation. One for the armed robbery charge, did two years for that. One for violating a restraining order, did a week for that and paid the fifteen thousand dollar fine. I'm emailing you his sheet now."

Where the hell was Jane while her father served his time?

"What about her mother?"

"April Morgan."

Jane Morgan.

Jane was using her mother's last name.

"Where is she?"

"Died in childbirth. No arrests. Married to Carl for less than two years when she died. That's all I have on her."

"Where in Montana is Carl?"

"Fucking hell," Rhode ground out. "Fucking, motherfucker—"

"What?"

"Jane's father isn't a biker; he's the king fucking biker. There's been movies made about his club and not the fluffy documentary kind about bikers who do good for their communities, the major motion picture kind about rivalry and war. Satan is the president of the Montana chapter of Ares Motorcycle Club."

'Fucking hell' didn't cover what a colossal issue this was.

The Ares was on the Justice Department's list of the top four deadliest motorcycle gangs in the US. At last count their membership, including the support clubs, rivaled the number of active HA members.

"It's starting to make sense," Rhode put in.

"What is?"

"Zeus. The Horsemen. Ares is the son of Zeus and Hera, the Greek god of war. The horses of Ares, the four horses of the apocalypse—the Horsemen."

"Are you turning into Cole? How the hell do you know this?"

Cole Keniston was Takeback's resident sage. He could spout off some obscure philosophical theory, or recite a poem, or quote the Buddha at the drop of a hat.

"Google."

Well, that explained Rhode's sudden mythology expertise.

"While you're at it why don't you Google how the hell we're going to neutralize Jane's father."

There was a beat of silence that told me I wasn't going to like what Rhode had to say.

"I'll talk to Wilson, but, Davis, this might not be something we can fix without starting a war we might not be able to win. We're talking Ares, not the Horsemen. They span all over the world. If the president of a chapter wants his daughter, he's going to have the support of the entire club. You know this culture. Jane's unclaimed. She's Satan's property."

Satan's property.

Christ.

That made my stomach roil.

"I'll claim her."

"Say again?"

I understood my friend's shock. I was still reeling from the stupidity of my suggestion, but actually that might work.

"I'll claim her," I said with more conviction. "I'll marry her."

"Dude, I get you trying to protect her. I don't want to see Carl get his hands on her any more than you do. Wilson will feel the same. We're in the business of rescuing women, not handing them over to men who want to do them harm. But again, we're not talking about the Horsemen. And you're not in that life—I'm not sure you marrying her is going to matter to an outlaw motorcycle gang."

Rhode was right. Marrying Jane wouldn't offer her much protection, but it was still going to happen.

"I'm marrying her and we'll go from there."

"Please, for the love of God, don't marry the woman."

"We'll get it—"

"Seriously. If you marry Jane, you realize that my woman's head will pop off and spin around in circles. First Reese and Sadie, then Letty and River when we've been planning our wedding the longest. If you're really going to do this, I'm taking Brooklyn to the courthouse this afternoon."

As Rhode spoke, I walked to the window and looked out at the beautiful beach.

"You should make that appointment, Rhode. I plan on marrying Jane by this evening."

"Does Jane have a say in this fucked-up plan of yours?"

Sure she did, as long as her answer was yes.

"She'll see it my way," I lied, knowing damn, good, and well Jane was going to fight me tooth and nail.

For some reason I liked the thought of Jane pitching a fit.

She was unlike any woman I'd ever been attracted to. I liked shy, quiet women. Not subservient but reserved.

Jane Morgan was not reserved; she was hot-headed when pushed.

Oh, yeah, this was going to be fun.

"I gotta go talk to Jane," I told Rhode and went to the dresser to get my kit.

"What about Zeus?"

I opened the adjoining door to the room next to mine and stared at the still-closed door that led to Jane's room.

"Fuck Zeus."

With that I hung up and went to work picking the lock that would open the door to my soon-to-be-wife's room.

The fuck of it was, I felt no hesitation.

CHAPTER FOUR

"Are you insane?" I asked and threw my hands out before I realized I was the one who probably looked insane as I flailed my arms like a toddler throwing a tantrum. I settled my hands on my hips before I continued. "First you break into my room. Then you tell me we're getting married."

As cool as a man could be who had lost his mind, Davis nodded.

"Though you forgot the part where I told you I knew who your father was."

"Right, Davis, and that makes you *more* insane. My father is worse than my brother. He won't care I'm married to an outsider. Hell, he wouldn't care if I was an old lady. He'd make the order to have me released and no one would dare to go up against him. This won't work."

Davis shrugged.

I stared.

What the infuriating man didn't do was speak.

"Seriously—"

"Listen, Jane, you're right. Us getting married won't solve the problem but it's a start."

Now I knew for sure Davis had lost his mind.

Either that or he knew nothing about motorcycle club culture.

"No, Davis, it's not a start. I'm telling you Satan won't care. Not only that but us being married will only draw attention to you."

"Exactly."

Exactly?

That was it, just one word with no further rationalization.

"You're going to have to explain that to me. No one, and I mean no one, wants to be on my father's radar."

"Why don't we sit?"

My gaze went from Davis standing in front of the window blocking my beautiful view of the ocean to the only surface I could sit on unless I was going to hike myself up on the dresser.

The bed.

If I'd known a crazy man was going to rent the adjoining room, pick the lock, and help himself to my personal space I would've reserved a suite with a sitting area. However, since I couldn't predict my current dilemma I booked the smallest room in the hotel. And there was no way I was getting any closer to the bed while Davis was in my room.

"I'm good where I am." I paused to add, "Though if you're uncomfortable standing you could go back to your room so I could finish packing."

Unfazed, Davis went on, "We need to talk about this."

Exasperated, I couldn't stop my hands from coming off my hips and flying out to my sides. I probably looked like a deranged prairie chicken trying to take flight with my arms flaying as they were but in that moment I couldn't bring myself to care that I was making an ass out of myself in front of the very-good-looking-though-certifiably-insane Davis Wright.

"There is nothing to talk about. I already told you, calling

Takeback was a mistake. I don't want your help and I'm absolutely not going to marry you."

"So, you're what, just going to hope your dad doesn't find you? Maybe move around until you run out of money? Or will Zeus be funding your expedition?"

Ugh.

"I get you think I condone my brother's business practices but I don't. I have never accepted money from my brother and I never will."

Davis's brows pulled together and that frown I was beginning to think was his signature look was firmly back on his stupidly handsome face.

"Business practices," he spat. "Is that what you call blackmail and selling drugs? What about the women he pimps out? What do you call that, his side hustle?"

I didn't need to be told that my brother had turned into a foul, lowlife criminal. Though I was sick of being reminded.

"No, Davis, I call that disgusting. I also call it none of my business because I am in no way a part of his world. I can't stop him from doing what he does any more than I can stop my father from being a piece of shit. The only thing I can do is what I do—stay away from them and mind my own damn business."

The wrinkles around his eyes softened, which only annoyed me more. One minute it was clear he thought I was just as bad as my family, then the next minute he looked almost like he felt bad for me.

Before he had a chance to insult me again I went on. "I don't get you. You obviously don't like me, so I'm confused as to why you'd want to help me."

"I don't not like you. I don't know you."

The absurdity of the conversation hit me. Nervous laughter bubbled up until I couldn't hold it back, and I busted into what I was sure sounded like delirious giggles.

"You…you…you…" I stammered, unable to get more out.

"Me, what?" Davis asked when I didn't finish.

It took more time than it should've before I was able to quell my laughter.

"You don't know me," I finally said. "Yet you want to marry me."

Davis looked like he was going to say something but stopped and narrowed his eyes on the door across the room. Then lightning fast—I mean, superhero fast—he was suddenly in front of me and pulling me toward the door to his room, snatching my purse off the dresser as he went. I didn't protest this mainly because I couldn't. He was closing the doors and locking the one on his side before my mouth had time to process what had happened.

"What—"

"Shh."

"Davis—" The last syllable came out muffled because the asshole had his hand over my mouth.

After that I understood why.

It wasn't like the walls were paper thin, but it was a hotel and not a very expensive one. It was easy to hear someone was in my room, and not being quiet about it.

"She's not fucking here."

There were a few seconds of silence before the man in my room went on, "Trust me, I know, Prez. I was nice the first time. I didn't think the bitch had it in her. I won't be nice this time."

My eyelids drifted closed as reality set in.

The man who my father sent to Idaho to pick me up was in Hawaii. And he was right, he had been nice in an asshole-biker sort of way. In other words, he could've been more of a prick when he told me my father wanted me home and he didn't want to hear any backtalk from me or he'd duct tape my mouth.

Davis's hand dropped but only as far as my shoulder. He squeezed twice, which I was positive was meant to be reassuring but it did nothing to calm my fear.

Once again, my father was going to get his way.

Only this time, it would be me, not Trevor who paid the price.

If only marrying Davis would fix my problem, I'd be at the altar so fast my hair would catch fire.

Unfortunately, a piece of paper and a few promises to God wouldn't deter Satan.

CHAPTER FIVE

Jane was trembling.

Not just her shoulders but her whole body was shaking.

Fear so thick I was shocked it wasn't choking her as it spilled out with every shallow puff of air she exhaled. Fear that couldn't be faked or mistaken for anything other than what it was—pure terror. Fear that pissed me right the fuck off and confused me.

What woman—or man for that matter—refused help when what they were up against scared them so badly they trembled from head to toe? But that was exactly what Jane had done—flatly refused the out I'd given her.

"No, Prez." I heard through the wall, grateful the idiot had zero clue how to be covert. "Don't call that motherfucker yet. If the bitch didn't already give him a heads up, I want my visit to be a surprise."

At that, Jane stopped shaking and turned to stone.

My guess, the bitch was Jane and the motherfucker was Zeus.

The biker in the next room got one of the two correct—Zeus was a motherfucker. But for some reason beyond me not being fond in general of men calling women bitches, hearing him referring to *Jane* as a bitch set my blood boiling.

This had nothing to do with her reaction and everything to do with a place inside of me I was doing my best to ignore. A place that would lead down a path that would be disastrous. Yet it couldn't be denied I felt something for the woman standing in front of me that went beyond disgust that she was the sister of a piece-of-shit loser.

The door slammed.

Jane jolted.

My blood, already boiling, turned to lava.

"He found me," she whispered.

I pinched my lips in an effort not to remind her I'd already told her that was going to happen. I, however, didn't think a biker would get on a plane and fly over the Pacific to make a pick-up. I figured he'd nab her when she flew back to the mainland.

"I have to…" she petered out then repeated, "I have to…"

Again she didn't finish her statement but she did try to step back.

I wasn't ready to lose the contact, even if that was just my hand on her shoulder. So when Jane attempted to move away I curled my fingers deeper and shook my head.

"*We*," I corrected. "We have to regroup. Let me call this in to the office then we'll plan how we're going to get you out of this hotel."

Jane jerked out of my hold while shaking her head.

"No, Davis—"

"Yes, Jane."

"Davis—"

"Give me one reason," I cut her off again. "One reason why I should walk away when less than two minutes ago you were so scared you were shaking. Or better yet tell me why you'd rather take your chances going at this alone—with the possibility of you getting nabbed high and be taken back to your father where you'd live the rest of your life wishing you were dead—than accept my help."

Something I couldn't read because I didn't know her sparked in her eyes. It wasn't fear, I'd seen her afraid. It wasn't anger because I'd seen that, too. This was something altogether different.

"You don't understand," she quietly murmured.

"Understand what?"

"What it's like being me."

The obvious answer to that was she was correct—I didn't know her personally so I had no clue what her life had been like to understand her as a person. Though I had a suspicion her meaning went deeper than that.

"So explain it to me."

There was a stretch of silence while her gaze darted around my room. It was identical to hers right down to the art on the walls. She was buying time. But the longer the silence went on, the more I started to doubt she was going to answer, until she straightened her shoulders and pinned me with her gaze.

"Actually, I shouldn't have to explain it to you of all people," she began, her voice edging to anger. "Earlier you did what all people do when they find out Trevor is my brother. They paint me with the same brush, thinking they know me, then do exactly what you did, and judge me. When I was a kid, it was the parents. When I was in junior high, it was my class-mates and parents. By the time I hit high school, it was my classmates, teachers, parents, *and* the town. There was nowhere I could go where I wasn't Satan's daughter. I was an outcast, dirty, a biker bitch in the making. I'd amount to nothing. I was guilty by association and not one single person took the time to get to know me. I was what my father was and that was it." Jane paused and frowned. "Same for Trevor. He didn't stand a chance. He had it worse than I did in a lot of ways. But instead of doing what I did, he proved them right. He became our father. Only in his stupidity he decided to one-up Satan."

I felt my lips curl in disgust.

"Are you seriously trying to justify what your brother—"

"See, that right there. You're quick to judge."

"I'm not judging you, Jane. It sounds to me like you're making excuses for your brother."

Without missing a beat, Jane leaned in, jabbed a finger in my direction, and snarled, "Of course it sounds that way to you, because you're a judgmental asshole who's made up his mind and can't fathom there is a difference between an explanation and an excuse. You think you have it all figured out but in reality you know nothing. You don't know me. You don't know Trevor or why he is the way he is. And before you say it, I've already heard it; it doesn't matter why he does what he does. But it does. It matters. If you don't understand the whys and the motivation behind his quest to be the biggest dick he can possibly be you'll never understand that he will not back down. You'll never understand that his endgame is death. That's the only way he bests my father—to go down in a blaze of glory. My brother will never go to jail, he will die first. He will orchestrate his death, he'll force you to kill him. His only goal in life is to show up my father."

Jane wasn't entirely wrong. However, I didn't need to understand his childhood to know the man he'd become. And if that was me being judgmental so be it. Zeus's reign of terror was coming to an end and it didn't matter why he was the way he was. The only thing that mattered was he needed to be stopped.

"What does this have to do with you and why you're hell-bent on giving your father what he wants?"

"*I* will die before I go back to my father."

Jesus Christ.

She meant that.

"So, you'd rather die than accept help from me," I noted.

"I would rather take my chances than be treated like a dirty—"

"You are *not* a dirty anything," I cut in, my temper starting to flare. "And at no point have I treated you like you were."

"No, Davis, you've treated me like everyone else does when they find out who my family is. But see, I'm not a little girl starving for attention. I'm not a teenager who desperately wants to fit in and have friends. I have long since discovered who *I* am." Jane pointed at herself. "Me. Jane. I am not who they said I was. I know my heart. I know my worth and I do not allow anyone to punish me for losing in the parent lottery. I am not either of them and I will be damned if you or anyone else judges me for anything other than my actions."

I'm not a little girl starving for attention.

Fuck, but I knew what that was like.

After my father left, my mom had done her best. She'd worked two, sometimes three jobs to keep a roof over our heads and food on the table—meaning I rarely saw her when she wasn't dog-ass tired. I knew better than to ask her for anything and that included her time.

It seemed the Lawrence siblings had one thing in common —they'd die to prove a point. I was still unclear what Zeus's point would be other than proving he was a total moron asshole who had not shown his father up but the opposite— he'd become the man he obviously didn't like. That was just plain stupid. Jane—now her, I understood. Being traded for her father's debt would mean ugly things for her. A living nightmare. One I could help prevent if she wasn't so stubborn.

My phone vibrated in my pocket and as shitty as the timing was I had to take it.

I pulled my phone out, saw it was my boss Wilson McCray, and took the call.

"Yeah?"

"Rhode ran some names," Wilson got straight to the point. "Luke James, enforcer for the Ares MC, bought a ticket to Honolulu. He should've landed an hour ago."

"I think he's already at the hotel." I looked at Jane and asked, "Luke James?" I relayed the name. "Is that who was in your room?"

"I only know his road name,"

I went back to Wilson. "You hear that?"

"Yeah. Chopper," he answered, not sounding surprised I was with Jane, nor that we'd already been paid a visit.

"Chopper."

I didn't need a verbal confirmation; her eyes widening and her head bobbing was enough.

"That's him," I told Wilson. "Did he come alone?"

"As far as we know, yes. But, Rhode's only ran the officers. Not the members. And seeing as the chapter Satan is the president of is triple the Horsemen, it'll take a while."

Fuck. This was not ideal, though Wilson already knew that so I didn't comment.

"I've arranged a flight to Lanai for you and Jane. You have a room at the Four Seasons."

"Damn, brother, you win the lottery?"

"Something like that," he grumbled.

I made a mental note to ask him about that comment later.

"When do we leave?"

"It's private, so whenever you get there. Though the sooner the better. I've emailed you Rhode's report and texted you a picture of Chopper."

Right on cue, my phone vibrated in my hand.

"Great. We'll leave now. Text me the airport and flight info."

"Already done."

Another text vibrated and I ended the call. "I'll text you when we're on the plane."

Wilson didn't bother with a sign off, he simply disconnected. I lowered my phone and pulled up the text and got my first look at the man who was trying to take Jane. I tapped the screen to enlarge the image and the man was not what I was expecting. If I didn't know he was a biker and he wasn't wearing an Ares cut I wouldn't have guessed he was in an MC. The guy was decent looking, close-cropped beard, short hair, graying on the sides. His white tee under his cut was clean, jeans the same, and the boots on his feet were worn but not worn out. He looked like every other mountain man I'd met in Idaho and Montana. If you didn't know who he was you could easily mistake him for a respectable, everyday guy.

I held my phone out and faced the screen toward Jane.

"This him?"

Once again her facial expression answered for her.

"Yeah."

I thought I'd put the pieces together, but still asked, "How'd he get to you? I mean, the first time in Idaho."

"He knocked on my front door and I opened it. He wasn't wearing his cut."

That tracked.

I could see Jane innocently opening the door to this man—a biker in a cut, especially one bearing her father's colors, no way. She'd be smarter than that.

"You can tell me the rest on the plane. We—"

"I'm not going," she stubbornly returned.

I'd had enough.

The woman was impossibly hardheaded.

"Check this, Jane, you've got two options. One, you walk out of here on your own two feet and I get you safe. Or, I cuff you and carry you out of here and get you safe. I don't give the first fuck which you pick, but one way or another you're coming with me."

Jane crossed her arms and scowled. I was sure the scowl was meant to convey anger. However, the pout on her lips was cute as hell and in no way intimidating.

"So, what you're saying is not only do I have one man trying to kidnap me but two."

"You can call it whatever you want. You can also kick and scream and throw a shit fit all the way to the plane. As I said, it makes no difference to me."

"You're impossible," she griped.

"Back atcha, sister."

Jane held my eyes and we went into a stare down. I'd give her to the count of thirty before I tossed her over my shoulder and did what I told her I would do. It would suck having to carry her out of the hotel kicking and screaming; the attention that would draw would make it impossible to slip out unnoticed. However, I'd have her to the airport before the police could arrive.

"Why?" she whispered.

On the surface that question was easy. This was what I did, what my job was, what I'd been called to do. I couldn't imagine doing anything else. However, with Jane it ran deeper. The thought of her father getting his hands on her didn't make my gut roil with disgust—it pierced my heart. The thought actually scared the fuck out of me. Another reaction to her I was actively ignoring.

I decided on the easy answer.

"You know what Takeback does. You know who I am. Do you really think I'm the type of man who would leave you to fend for yourself when I can make you safe?"

"I don't know what type of man you are, beyond infuriating."

"Right. Only you would think it's infuriating I insist on saving your ass."

Then since I needed this conversation to end, I ended it and did it in a way it would be done—for good.

"You can think whatever the fuck you want about me, Jane. Like you, I long ago stopped caring about other people's opinions of me. Though I think for me it ended sooner seeing as it was sometime in the fifth grade when my mom and I had to sleep on my aunt's couch for about a month. Since my aunt wasn't thrilled to have to put up her sister and nephew she pitched a fit about how much water we were using. Which meant I did what I could to stop the shrill bitch from complaining and only took one shower a week. And since you experienced something similar though very different I don't need to tell you that kids are dicks. They noticed, made comments, and talked shit. It was then I learned none of them cared my mom was working her ass off. No one gave a shit we were homeless and I was already going through shit at home and I didn't need more when I was at school. In turn I learned not to give a fuck what anyone thought about me or my mom because none of them knew why we were where we were. So, to end this stupid argument once and for all, you can think whatever the fuck you want to think about me. Call me judgmental, infuriating, an asshole, bossy, controlling, whatever you can think up. Because at the end of the day, I know who *I* am, what *I* stand for, and I'm doing the right thing. So what will it be, Jane? Are you walking out of here or am I dragging you out? You got two seconds to decide."

With that I picked up my backpack off the bed.

Thankfully she made the right decision and grabbed her purse off the dresser.

"I'll walk out."

CHAPTER SIX

Davis walked out first which was good since my mind was still spiraling from what he'd told me.

Homeless.

With all the dysfunction and filth I'd grown up around I'd never been worried about where I was going to sleep. I'd never had to forgo showers because someone was complaining about the water bill. No, when I skipped a shower it was either because I didn't have time to clean it before I got in—which was a necessity when you had an older brother who was always covered in dirt and grease and didn't care when he left the remnants of that all over the shower—or it was because one or more club sluts had spent the night and used the shower and there was no way I was chancing getting in and catching a skin-eating fungus from one of them.

My brother was dirty.

Club sluts were altogether a different kind of dirty that would require cream and antibiotics to get rid of their filth.

I was still silently lost in my head when Davis led us to the stairs. I still hadn't sorted myself as we descended then pushed through the door to the lobby. I was just getting my bearings as we approached the exit.

Then suddenly, without warning my back was against the wall, Davis's face was inching closer to mine, then his lips were on mine.

His lips…

On mine…

Closed mouth and hard.

Any wits I'd managed to get under control fled.

I was now lost in a new mind-bending way with his hard body pressing against me and his scent surrounding me. My eyes closed, my brain forgot we didn't like him, and my body came alive. All of this happened in a matter of seconds, so fast I couldn't stop the tingling that started at my neck and traveled down my chest until my breasts felt heavy and my nipples hardened.

Not good.

Really, *really* not good.

It took a turn for the worse when Davis lifted his hand and cupped my jaw.

Oh, yeah, this was way, *way* worse now that his calloused palm held me captive, deterring any chance I had to pull myself together.

I wanted to push him away or pull him closer or open my mouth and take the kiss someplace else or knee him between his legs for being such a prick. The problem was my mind was a jumbled mess of lust and dislike and I couldn't make up my mind which one I wanted to do more.

Lust was quickly winning out when Davis pulled back just a fraction and whispered, "Just go with it."

"Go with what?" I managed to ask before his mouth hit mine, this time taking it in a scorching open-mouth kiss.

Holy…

Fucking…

Shit.

Davis didn't start off slow like most men I'd kissed. He didn't bother with tentative first touches of tongues—the get-to-know-you part of the kiss if you will. Nope. Not Davis. He was too self-assured for all that. He just went for it. Confident. Bold. Commanding. He left me no choice but to follow his lead. Any further questions or protests—I *really* should've been protesting—were impeded by the moan that had worked its way up from my belly and spilled into his mouth. Davis heard it and took the kiss deeper.

Oh. My. God.

The man was good. Given enough time, he could probably make me orgasm from his kiss alone.

Not good.

The worst.

I needed this to stop before I did something insane like rub up against him or worse, hop up and wrap my legs around his waist and beg him to take me back up to my room and show me if he was good with his tongue on other places of my body.

Fortunately he broke the kiss before that could happen.

Unfortunately I mewled in disappointment.

My eyes came open and I saw Davis's head was turned to the side, eyes scanning the lobby.

Right. Shit, we were in public.

Without a word he stepped away from me, grabbed my hand, and gave it a tug.

We were out of the building like it was on fire and we'd been told to evacuate.

Next thing I knew he was hoisting me into the passenger seat of a topless, doorless Jeep Wrangler. It was cool as hell and I wondered why I hadn't rented a kickass beach Jeep instead of the boring sedan.

Because you always play it safe, the good-girl angel on my shoulder reminded me.

Safe is boring. We need to have some fun, the not-so-good-girl angel on my other shoulder complained.

"Buckle up," Davis said, ending the imaginary conversation I was having with my conscience.

I did as told and watched Davis round the hood. His gaze was on the front of the hotel, expression unreadable, long legs moving at a fast clip.

He was in a hurry. No surprise, seeing as my hotel room had been invaded.

Before he got in, he pulled his phone out of his back pocket and tossed it to me. I barely caught it before it bounced off my lap, then the next thing I knew Davis was backing out of the parking spot. It's worth noting, he didn't bother with his seat belt. He just hopped in, fired up the Jeep, and went.

We were out of the parking lot when he said, "Pull up the text from Wilson and look up the address he sent."

"Are you going to buckle up?" I asked as I swiped the screen of his phone.

"Jane—"

"We're in a Jeep with no roof or doors." I told him something he very well knew as I found the text.

"Address," he barked.

I didn't like that—like at all.

One of the many promises I'd made to myself when I'd escaped my father and his club was I would never again allow a man to bark orders at me. Or make me feel that because I had a vagina I was somehow less than, or more to the point —subservient.

Fuck that noise.

"You either ask nicely or I throw your phone out the..." There was no window so I quickly amended, "Out of the Jeep."

Davis took his eyes off the road to skewer me with a stare.

I was immune. All my life, men bigger than him, scarier

than him, meaner, nastier, stared me down or gave me dirty looks as they ordered me around.

Davis Wright was a pussy cat compared to what I was used to.

"If you're going to look at me and not where you're going you really should have on your seat belt so when you crash you don't fly out of the vehicle and die. Your boss already hates me; I don't need him hating me more if you die because of your irresponsibility!" I yelled over the wind.

"Has anyone ever told you you're a pain in the ass?"

"My whole life," I answered honestly. "Actually those might've been my father's first words to me."

Davis's frown softened. Actually it didn't just soften, pity infused.

Fuck that, too.

I didn't need or want anyone's pity.

It was not my upbringing. I was not some scared, scarred woman who needed someone to tell me how sorry they were I'd been treated like dog shit my whole childhood.

It might've taken me years, but I was well beyond that shit.

"Put your seat belt on, Davis, and I'll give you the damn address."

Much to my surprise his gaze went back to the road and he buckled up.

It was then I rattled off the address.

Then I remained silent the rest of the ride with my eyes glued to the road in front of us trying to get my thoughts in order.

I needed to ask him about that kiss and tell him he was never to do it again. After that, I needed to figure out what I was going to do.

Now more than ever I had to get away from Davis and his wicked tongue.

I'D NEVER SEEN the inside of a private jet which obviously meant I'd never stepped foot inside of one. And I wished I still never had, seeing as all future commercial flights would seem like I was being stuffed into a cattle trailer.

I didn't have a fancy bone in my body. I drove an average car, I lived in a small two-bedroom average condo, my work clothes were decent but came from secondhand consignment shops, my regular kickabout clothes were just that—comfortable and not stylish. I owned no jewelry, save a ring I found that belonged to my mother. But I never wore it, not only because it was the only thing I had of hers and was afraid I'd lose it but also because turquoise and silver wasn't my jam.

Fancy or not, I couldn't deny flying in a private jet was awe-inspiring. No shuffling to get down the aisle, no waiting for other passengers to board, no cramming your bag in the overhead compartment, and no fighting for a window seat.

I waited until we'd taken off and the plane was gaining altitude before I asked, "Why'd you kiss me back at the hotel?"

"Chopper was in the lobby, walking to the elevators."

"So you kissed me?"

"Seemed like the best way to hide you from him."

I was attempting to shove the disappointment to the side while at the same time trying to figure out if it was fear or gratitude I was feeling.

"I thought you saw him," Davis continued.

Now, that was a reality check. I hadn't seen the man who was trying to abduct me in order to bring me to my father so he could trade me for a debt because I was too lost in my head. Another reason to get away from Davis as soon as possible. He threw me off my game. I knew better than to walk around like a mindless twit.

"I missed him," I admitted.

Davis was staring at me like he was expecting me to say more. I would never offer up the reason why I'd been so careless. I'd never tell him that my heart had cracked when he told me he and his mother were homeless. The man was already a jerk, God knows what he'd be like if he knew I was so distracted by what he'd told me I'd missed something important.

"What?" I prompted.

"Nothing."

Davis's eyes went to the tiny window and he stared out, thus ending our conversation.

I was grateful.

No, I wasn't. I was disappointed he hadn't scolded me, which would've served as a reminder he didn't like me. It was easy to forget when he unnecessarily helped me up the stairs of the plane with his hand on my lower back. It was easy to forget when he allowed me to pick my seat first then asked the attendant to get me a bottle of water as if sensing I was dying of thirst. It was especially easy to forget when Davis's mouth was on mine and he'd given me the best kiss of my life. Though I'd never tell him that.

"Where are we going?"

I saw his lips twitch but he quelled his smile before it formed.

"Lanai."

"And that's funny because?"

"Not funny," he started. "Amusing that you're just now asking where we're going."

Gah.

He had a point.

I should've asked back in the hotel room.

"I had other things on my mind."

"Such as?"

Damn, he was maddening.

"Such as you taking me against my will," I lamely retorted.

"If you say so."

This was perfect. This was exactly what I needed to wipe that kiss from my memory.

"And don't ever kiss me again."

I watched in horror as a full-blown, cocky smile tipped up Davis's perfect lips. A smile so full of arrogance that I knew I'd shown him my hand. He knew I enjoyed that kiss and more he knew it was still on my mind since I'd now mentioned it twice.

"Right," he muttered through his smile.

I really wanted to ask him about his sarcastic answer but instead I peeled my gaze from his and watched as we climbed higher and higher above the ocean. It was the smart thing to do, retreat to my corner and stop giving him ammunition to push my buttons.

I seriously had to regroup. I had to get myself and my situation under control and be smart.

"Well, that's disappointing," Davis mumbled.

"What is?" I asked the window.

"I didn't take you for a woman who backed down," he provoked.

Two could play this game.

"I see you're still jumping to conclusions about me. Did it occur to you that maybe I'm just done with the conversation and would rather not talk to you?"

"Nope, that's not why."

Cocky bastard.

I lasted three seconds before my curiosity got the better of me.

"Say I was backing down—which I'm not—why would that be disappointing?"

Davis was silent.

This went on so long it began to irritate me. I turned my

gaze back to him to find him intently studying me in a way that made me want to squirm in the plush leather seat.

"Davis?" I prompted.

He blinked, pulling out of his perusal, and shook his head as if he were trying to knock some vision loose.

"Just is."

"Now who's backing down?" I commented.

He didn't rise to the bait. He didn't make a single comment, snarky or otherwise.

His face went perfectly blank when he looked back out the window.

I should've been happy.

What I was, was disappointed and I wasn't sure what that said about me.

CHAPTER SEVEN

Thirty minutes later when we touched down in Lanai I could barely remember the details of the reports Wilson had sent me. In an effort to ignore Jane's presence I'd read them over twice. An effort that was for naught. The words all blended together on the screen as thoughts of that kiss invaded my mind. Then there was her attitude—both the stubborn side and the part where she knew her worth and wasn't afraid to put voice to who she knew she was. It was that side of her that almost had me convinced she disagreed with her brother's activities yet still defended him. The contradiction put me in a tough spot, and had me fighting double time to keep my curiosity at bay.

Jane was the opposite of the women I was normally attracted to. I liked shy women. The quiet ones who took hard work to get. Women who when they finally opened up and felt comfortable to be who they wanted to be made me know I'd won something special. I was careful with the women I'd dated, slow to move a relationship to anything intimate. I had a mind to the type of women I liked and they were not the type who gave of their bodies or time unless they knew it was going somewhere. That's not to say I hadn't had a few one-night stands but that was not my norm.

Jane was not shy or quiet. Though I did get the sense she guarded her time, body, and thoughts to the point she'd rather live out her days alone than have to trust a man to take care of the gifts she had to give.

Yet, from the moment we'd started exchanging barbs I wanted her. After that kiss I wanted to haul her back up to the hotel room, strip her naked, and fuck the hell out of her. So spending forty minutes with her on a private plane, I was fighting the urge to kiss her again instead of memorizing the details of her father's MC or the details of the man who was in Hawaii to abduct her.

Then there was the utterly silent twenty-minute drive to the Four Seasons. Not one peep from Jane, not even when a luxury SUV pulled onto the private runway and I ushered her into the back. Nothing as we drove through some of the most beautiful undisrupted countryside I'd ever seen. Not a house in sight. Mountains to one side and wide-open plains on the other.

The difference between Honolulu and Lanai was drastic. Pure beauty as far as the eye could see. And that beauty magnified when the ocean appeared in the distance and only got better the closer we got to the hotel.

The drive was silent.

My thoughts were not.

"Welcome to the Sensei Lanai," the driver said as he rolled to a stop in front of the hotel.

Scratch that.

This was paradise.

A luxury resort the likes of me should never step foot in. It was also a place where Luke James would immediately garner the attention of security. As it was, Jane and I would stick out like the intruders we were. However, knowing Wilson he would've already had appropriate clothes sent to our room.

"Mr. McCray has already called ahead," the driver continued, confirming my thoughts. The man turned slightly and bent his arm back, dangling two black wrist bands on his finger. "Your room keys."

I took the keys but before I had a chance to thank him or ask what instructions Wilson had given the hotel he began again.

"As instructed you're on the second floor, corner room near the emergency exit, jungle view. You're checked in. Mr. McCray asked for a resort map, complete with the gardens and pathways to be delivered to your room. You'll find those as well as the contact information for Miss Lise Fisher. She's your personal concierge and has been briefed. You will have total privacy during your stay. Again welcome to the Sensei, Mr. and Mrs. Wright. We hope you enjoy your stay with us."

With that he exited the car, leaving Jane staring at me with wide eyes.

"Just go with it," I mumbled as the driver opened her door.

"Last time I did that, you kissed me," she said under her breath and stepped out of the SUV.

It was good to know I wasn't the only one still thinking about that kiss.

"Thank you," Jane said and took the man's outstretched hand.

"Mr. McCray insisted on the back entrance to the hotel," the driver weirdly stated and held up a vibrant purple and white orchid lei. Jane awkwardly lowered her head and the man brightly added, "E komo mai."

Her eyes came to me and I shrugged at her unasked question.

"Thank you."

I swallowed a laugh as her thanks came out more of a question than appreciation.

"It's not a proper welcome unless you've been given a lei."

Rightly the driver assumed I didn't wish to be lei'd—at least not by him—and motioned to the entrance.

"Through there, elevators are to your left."

I reached into my back pocket to pull out my wallet when the driver stopped me, "That's not necessary, Mr. Wright. Mr. McCray has taken care of everything."

What the hell?

Since when did Wilson pay for expensive hotels and gratuity? I wouldn't call him cheap, but even on the government's dime we never stayed anywhere that wouldn't be considered a three-star hotel.

"Appreciate all your help."

I glanced back at Jane to find her taking in the garden. I had to admit it was something to see with giant statues mingled in the lush foliage.

"Maybe later we can walk the paths if you're interested."

Jane startled as if she'd forgotten I was standing right next to her.

"Yeah, sure."

I adjusted my backpack and double checked she had her purse then grabbed her elbow to guide her up the stairs. Surprisingly she didn't pull away. She also didn't speak as we walked into the lobby but came to an abrupt stop in front of a large sculpture that took pride of place in the middle of the very large space. Its mirrored polished finish seemed to clash with the warm welcoming feel of the atrium yet the beauty of the stainless-steel piece somehow worked.

"Aphrodite," Jane whispered.

I looked at the black freestanding name plate and it was indeed Aphrodite.

"How'd you know?"

Once again she startled. Though this time her face paled and she shook her head while saying, "My father is obsessed with Aphrodite. He has all sorts of pictures up of her around our house. He even has one in his office at the clubhouse."

Ah, that would explain her reaction. I was getting ready to steer us away from the statue when she shockingly shared more. "He wanted to name me Aphrodite. But my mother refused. His second choice was Kore."

"Kore?"

"Yes, as the myth goes Kore was the original name of Persephone who became the Queen of the Underworld after Hades abducted her. My mother didn't like that name either but compromised on Corinne, a variation of Kore. Of course I don't know if any of that is true seeing as my mother died before I got to meet her. So, the story could just be another one of my father's mind-fucks. When he told me that story it was my birthday, he was drunk, mourning the loss of his Queen like he did every year instead of celebrating my birthday so who knows? It could be total bullshit or the truth. I learned early on to take everything that comes out of his lying mouth with a grain of salt."

At Jane's confession, which I knew wasn't meant to be one but instead the story of how she got her name, I sucked in oxygen and held it in an effort to control the burning anger that had started in my gut and worked its way up to my chest and was fighting to escape.

Mourning the loss of his Queen like he did every year instead of cele-brating my birthday.

Growing up I had very little.

But I had a mother who loved me. Every year from as far back as I could remember my mom did something for my birthday even if it was one cupcake. She never let the day pass without making a big deal of it. Not with presents or a party—she smiled, she sang, she skipped around like my birthday was the best day of the year.

I would bet Jane had more than I had by way of material things.

But she had less.

No mother to sing happy birthday to her.

A piece of shit father who got drunk on her birthday.

Oh, yeah, my insides were boiling.

"I take it you don't like Aphrodite?" Jane asked.

"Huh?"

"You're staring at the statue like you want to—"

"I'm concentrating," I cut her off.

"On what?"

I blinked and the statue came back into focus before I slid my gaze to the beautiful woman standing next to me.

"Nothing," I lied.

Jane's gorgeous green eyes narrowed but before she could call me out I reached down and tagged her hand. "Come on."

Woodenly she walked to the elevator.

She was silent as we made our way to our room.

I opened the door, Jane walked in, and whirled on me as soon as the door was closed.

"Don't do that shit again," she snapped.

"Come again?"

"Lie to me."

I walked farther into the room asking, "When did I lie to you?"

"Downstairs. You said you were concentrating. I asked you on what and you said," Jane stopped, brought her hands up and made air quotes as she continued, "nothing. That was obviously a lie. If you're too chicken shit to tell me what you're thinking then say that. Don't treat me like I'm an idiot."

Right.

This was not about me blowing off a question I didn't want to answer. Hell, this wasn't about me at all. And knowing who her family was, it didn't take a psychologist to puzzle the pieces together but I still didn't like the accusation.

"Cool the attitude, Jane—"

"Please tell me you didn't just say that," she haughtily interrupted.

"Jesus," I muttered, remembering why I was single.

Women were fucking exhausting.

I shrugged off my pack and tossed it on the only bed in the room and looked around. A big comfortable-looking armchair in the corner that wasn't fit for sleeping and two wicker chairs out on the balcony.

One room.

One bed.

Jane was going to have another shit hemorrhage when she was done throwing this one and she realized she would be sharing a bed with me.

I should've guarded my smile.

I didn't and just as expected Jane asked, "What's funny?"

"I'd say *nothing* but I'm afraid your head will explode so I'll tell you with the preface, you asked so you can't get pissed when I tell you the answer."

Those fucking eyes that were going to be my downfall narrowed and her arms crossed over her chest.

"Christ, you're a pain in the ass." Then just because I wanted to push her buttons I tacked on, "A cute one, but still a pain in the ass."

She leaned in and growled, "Cute."

"Yup," I confirmed.

"You're unbelievable."

"Normally I don't hear that until after the first orgasm."

Jane's eyes went from tiny slivers to comically wide.

"That's some ego you got, Davis Wright."

"I can prove it to you—"

"I'll pass."

"You sure? I hear orgasms are——"

"Positive."

"Well, that's disappointing."

"That's me, one big, huge disappointment."

I stilled at her comment. All humor dissipated when I said, "I'm not sure if you're playing along with my joking or serious."

Jane said nothing.

I broke the silence.

"So that shit you said to me at the other hotel about knowing who you are, knowing your heart, knowing your worth was just that—shit. You were quick to call me judgmental but there you stand calling yourself a disappointment. What the fuck, Jane?"

"I know who I am," she quickly retorted.

"Then you'd know you could never be a disappointment."

Jane's gaze didn't just slide away, she turned her head fully toward the windows, cutting off eye contact.

I should've been grateful; the pain I saw before she averted her stare cut me to the quick.

What was it about her?

One minute I was happily exchanging verbal blows, the next I wanted to pull her into my arms and protect her from herself.

"Why are we talking about this?" she asked.

Was she fucking serious?

Instead of answering I brought the conversation back around. "There's one bed. That's what I was smiling about."

"So?"

"So?" I parroted.

"Yeah, so? You can sleep on the floor," she told me.

Right.

That wasn't going to happen.

I let that go, and went back to her original accusation.

"Just to clear the air, I don't think you're an idiot. Downstairs I didn't answer you because I was pissed."

At that her head whipped back and her eyes locked with mine.

"Pissed?"

"At your father, for being more of a dick than I already thought he was." The confusion on her face pissed me off more. "You really have no idea why that story you told me would make me angry?"

Jane shook her head.

That didn't piss me off. It pissed me way the fuck off.

"Your birthday?" I prompted and she shook her head again. "Baby, he was too drunk to celebrate your day."

"So? He never celebrated anything when it came to me and Trevor. The only time my father was happy was when he was with his MC doing whatever felonious shit they got up to. He hated us, especially me, so why would he celebrate anything that had to do with me?"

"Especially you?"

"Of course. I killed his Queen. He loathes my existence. Me breathing means my mother's not."

It felt like the floor beneath me gave way.

It wasn't Jane's pretty eyes that would be my downfall

It was the infuriating complexity that made her, her.

The beautiful woman who had multiple names, an outlaw for a brother, a father who was arguably worse, no mother to love her, and yet she still managed to carve out a decent life and be a good person.

Carl Lawrence didn't know the first thing about treating his woman like a queen.

But I sure as fuck did.

And Jane Morgan was going to learn what it meant to reign.

CHAPTER EIGHT

I needed to apologize. But after our intense conversation that ended when Davis told me to look through the bags of clothes that had been left for us while he excused himself to make a phone call on the balcony, I didn't know how.

I mean, I knew how to say the words, I'm sorry for acting like a crazy bitch. I just didn't know how to say it without having to explain why I'd behaved like a crazy bitch. Though he deserved the explanation along with the apology.

I seemed to have this horrible affliction when I was around Davis—I spoke too much. I said things I'd never told another soul. There was a reason why I changed jobs so frequently, I didn't want friends. Friends made you do things like share stories. They talked about the past and my past was off-limits. They talked about dreams and the future, neither of which I wanted to discuss. The former because I had none, the latter because it was depressing.

I hadn't lied. I knew who I was, my heart, and my worth. That didn't mean that every now and again when I allowed myself to think about certain things, my father's cruelty didn't tear me apart. It didn't mean that I didn't have moments of weakness, and telling Davis about how I got my name was a big, fat, honking moment of weakness. I never should've told him. That story left me vulnerable. I knew better. Trevor had drilled it into me since I was a child, never to allow anyone to have the upper hand. Never trust anyone with your secrets. Never let anyone close. In the thirty-five years since he'd explained to me how the world worked, I hadn't let a single person in.

I kept everyone at arm's length.

Until Davis.

Now I was spilling secrets left and right.

I heard the door open and realized in the time Davis had been outside I hadn't looked through the bags. I was still standing in the same spot I'd been in since we'd walked into the beautiful hotel room staring at the bed—the only bed.

Perhaps running off at the mouth wasn't the only thing I suffered from when I was around Davis. Time loss and rapid heart rate were also symptoms only he inflicted. If I was being totally honest, wet panties and hard nipples could be added to the list, however, I was all for pretending he had no effect over my body.

"I need to apologize," I blurted out.

Davis finished closing the door and gave me his attention.

Before I lost my nerve I told him the truth, which meant my mouth spoke more words, spilled more secrets, that didn't only leave me vulnerable but wide open.

"It was the statue. It was telling you that stupid story. It was remembering my father slurring his words as he told me he wanted to name me Aphrodite. It was hearing the pain in his voice when he spoke about my mother and the anger directed at me. I was a bitch to you when we got into the room and I lashed out because I was feeling raw. That's no excuse but it's why I said what I said to you. I'm sorry. You're entitled to your thoughts and you don't have to tell me what they are. You didn't lie to me, I was just acting crazy."

Davis stood perfectly still staring at me, which made more words that shouldn't have been said come out.

"And I know who I am. None of what I told you was bull-shit. I know I'm a good person. But that doesn't mean that every once in a while I don't feel their filth coat my skin. That doesn't mean that I don't remember where I came from and who my father is. I was raised by club skanks and my big brother before he turned into our father. Trevor was all I had. There was a time when I knew he loved me and he protected me from my father's brothers."

Now that I'd started I couldn't stop. I needed Davis to understand. I needed someone to understand. I needed to tell the truth. Not because it would absolve my brother but someone had to know why he was the way he was.

"He slept beside me so no one would sneak into my room in the middle of the night. He wouldn't let them touch me and when one tried he almost died protecting me. It was not the brother he disrespected who called the meeting. It was my father. *His* father who called the brothers to the table to vote on Trevor's punishment for protecting me. His little sister. I was thirteen and my father didn't see an issue with a man older than him…" I stopped to suck in much-needed oxygen before I spat out the rest. "Trying to force himself on me. My father, his father, didn't care that his teenage daughter was almost violated by his road captain and I would've been if Trevor hadn't come home when he did. Instead, Trevor was beaten by every patched member who wanted to take a swing at him. That doesn't make anything he does now right. It almost makes it worse because he knew what that did to me. He knew how scared I was. But that day, after that meeting, my loving older brother was gone. That day Trevor turned into Zeus. He made it known he'd slit any man's throat who dared to touch me. The next day he proved that true when my father's road captain was found dead and Trevor took off. After that no one tried again. My brother did that for me, not my father. I don't know Zeus, I don't want to know him, I can't know him. But I love my big brother."

When I was done Davis was still staring at me.

I said nothing. Mainly because I was panting, partly because I didn't know what else to say.

Now he knew.

Davis knew that Trevor had saved me from something that would've scarred me for the rest of my life and because of that he had my undying love.

Zeus, no.

Trevor, always.

"I need a minute, baby."

With that Davis turned, opened the door, and slammed it behind him.

I watched with no small amount of horror as Davis walked to the railing and dropped his head forward.

This time I'd said way too much. Things I couldn't take back but was having a hard time regretting them even though I knew Trevor would be angry I'd told his secret.

It might've been seconds or minutes or a really long time but the door opened and Davis came back into the room. I didn't need to see him entering, I could feel his presence. Overwhelming anger filled the room. So much I found it hard to take a full breath.

"First," he started and it sounded like a gunshot rent the air. "I'm sorry that happened to you. To say I'm glad your brother stopped it would be a gross understatement. And you're right, Jane, it makes what he does now worse because he does it to a woman who might not be his sister but they could be someone's sister. These women are someone's daughter. They are people who don't deserve what he does to them. I'm sorry if that hurts you, but it's the fucking truth. And seeing as he stopped his baby sister from being *violated*." That last was ground out like the filthy verb it was. "He damn well fucking has it in him to do right. As for your apology, I appreciate it. Not just the apology itself but you trusting me with the explanation."

Trust.

I'd never trusted anyone but Trevor and now I didn't trust him at all.

"Now since you gave me honesty, I'm gonna give you some," he continued. "Pretty much everything you tell me about your father and brother pisses me right the fuck off. So in the future when you tell me something and I need a minute to digest what motherfucking assholes they are, you need to understand it's no reflection on you. You came from where you came from. None of us can change that. It's *their* filth, and, baby, it doesn't coat you. You don't have a damn thing to hide or be ashamed of. If someone wants to judge you for your family and not see the strong, beautiful woman you are, fuck 'em. They aren't worth your time."

I wanted to believe that.

I really, *really* did. But just a few short hours ago, Davis was looking at me like I was one of them—scum, filth, a criminal.

Something had changed but I didn't want to know why or how it had. I needed to keep my distance. I needed to remember he was only there to help me with my father, then he'd leave and go back to his life and I'd have to find a new place to live. One that was far away from my brother, something I should've done years ago but was too scared. Even though Trevor was who he was, I still felt safe knowing he was close.

I had no one else.

"I talked to Wilson," Davis abruptly changed topics.

I didn't know what to say to that so I said nothing and

waited for an explanation. He didn't elaborate, instead he looked at the bags on the bed.

"Did you go through the bags?"

"No."

Davis made his way to the bed, grabbed a bag, and opened it, looked inside, then set it back down. He did this with three other bags before he obviously found the one he was looking for and rifled through it until he found what he wanted and tossed two boxes on the bed. One was rectangle and one looked a hell of a lot like a ring box. Then he went back to the bag and pulled out a tie and black dress socks.

"Your dress is hanging in the closet," he announced.

"Dress?"

"We're getting married."

I felt my breath leave my lungs in a whoosh, which made it impossible for me to protest. This was unfortunate because it gave Davis the opportunity to continue speaking.

"Wilson had a sit down with Zeus and laid out my plan. Your brother agrees. We get married tonight. Tomorrow your brother gets the word you're married and to whom. As you said, your father won't give the first fuck, until he looks into me and who I work for."

"My brother and Wilson had a sit down?" I asked.

"Yep."

I was sure Wilson McCray was not happy he'd had to sit across from my brother for any reason, but I was positive he was less happy to be doing it to discuss my problem, which had nothing to do with him or Takeback.

"And the two of them decided it was a good idea for me to marry you?"

"Yep."

"No, Davis, hear me…" I paused to reel in my temper. "My brother and your boss decided what was best for me without me being a part of that conversation."

"Us getting married solves—"

"That's not the point," I interrupted. "My brother doesn't get to make decisions on my behalf. Hell, he doesn't get a say in my life, period. I only went to him because I needed to get out of town quickly and he's the only criminal I know who could get me a fake ID and credit cards."

"So the other criminals you know weren't available?" he teased.

I felt my temper flaring and since I'd already made an ass out of myself I was trying extra, super hard not to act like a bitch again. It was a losing battle. I was too pissed.

"You think this is a joke?" I snapped. "I don't think it's amusing that decisions about my life are being made behind my back."

Davis was quiet for a moment before he shook his head. "No, Jane, I don't think any of this is a joke, especially the part where your father wants you taken back to Montana so he can trade you to pay off a debt. Hear *me*," Davis mocked. "Your father wants to trade *you*. I think it goes without me having to explain this, but your brother's not Wilson's favorite person. He's not mine. So it fucks me to say this, but he's right about this. Once your father finds out you're married to me and he sees I work for Takeback who has ties to law enforcement, including the feds, you become untouchable."

I hadn't thought about that when Davis first proposed his crazy plan.

And it sucked they were right.

But still…

"You might be right, but—"

"There's no *might* about it. I'm right. Rhode is right now laying a nice easy trail of information for your father and his idiot brothers to find. They won't even have to dig to find it."

I wondered if counting to ten really worked. I tried it and

found it didn't. So, I went to fifteen and was no less pissed when Davis called, "Jane?"

"Quiet, I'm counting."

"The ways to murder me in my sleep or…" He let that hang.

"If I was going to murder you, you'd be wide awake when I did it."

"Right," he mumbled through a grin.

Dick.

I let my gaze drop to the floor, this time not bothering to count but instead taking a deep breath.

Okay, this was fake.

The marriage would be on paper only.

I could do a fake marriage if it meant I was useless to my father.

I'd be untouchable, as Davis said.

Divorce was easy enough. It wouldn't be like a real marriage where love and feelings and finances were all tangled together. That was when it got messy.

I could marry the handsome Davis Wright, then divorce him and move on.

It was actually a fool-proof plan.

He'd never fall for someone like me and I sure as hell knew better than to fall for him.

Perfect.

Decision made, I lifted my head and looked at my soon-to-be-fake-husband.

"So, here are the rules," I started. "I participate in every decision that affects—"

"Nope."

"What do you mean, nope?"

"No, Jane. You don't participate in every decision when it comes to your safety. Actually, you have no say in that at all. Protection is quite literally my job. When it comes to your father and your brother and me keeping them from harming you in any way you have no say. That's nonnegotiable. And this is the last gift you accept from your brother."

I was now rethinking how easy this marriage was going to be.

"Gift? What are you talking about?"

"The private jet, the Four Seasons, this is all on your brother's dime."

I glanced around the beautiful room located in a luxury resort and I knew it had to cost thousands of dollars a night and that wasn't including the ride on the private jet. I couldn't begin to guess how much that cost.

Thousands and thousands of dollars Trevor got from drugs, prostitution, and God knew what else.

My stomach twisted in disgust.

"We're leaving," I announced.

"Come again?"

"We're leaving. Right now. We're not staying here, not with his money. Not the way he earned it. No fucking way, Davis."

"Jane—"

"*He hurts people*," I hissed. "I'm not staying here using his money knowing that someone was hurt so I could hide away in a crazy expensive hotel."

"Okay, baby. We'll find somewhere else."

Wait. What?

"We'll find somewhere else?"

"I'll call Wilson—"

"Just like that?"

Davis had been standing across the room. The space wasn't huge but it wasn't a Motel 6 either. I had plenty of time to watch him move to me. So that was what I did, I watched thinking I liked the way he carried himself. He was tall and built, his strides confident yet graceful. And when he stopped in front of me I had to tilt my head back to look at him.

I liked that his height made me feel safe. He could wrap his arms around me and cocoon me in his warmth.

I quickly shoved that dangerous thought away.

Though as soon as he lifted his hand, curled it around the side of my neck, and gently squeezed, the thought was back along with a trill of excitement that wasn't as easy to push aside.

"I'll call Wilson," he softly told me. "See if he can get the time of the wedding changed to earlier. After that we'll grab our shit and find someplace new to stay."

Okay, so, this fake marriage was absolutely not going to work. Not when Davis was being sweet while stroking the side of my throat.

"Am I overreacting?"

"Not for me to say."

His thumb continued to stroke, the feel of it familiar and intimate. Way too intimate for who we were yet I didn't step away. I stupidly stood there accepting his easy affection, and not only that, I soaked it up and let it settle the knot in my stomach.

"I asked," I reminded him.

"Okay, then how about this? You're entitled to feel however you feel. I can't say I disagree. This room was paid for by someone else's misery."

That was a nice thing for him to say. Too considerate actually. I needed Davis to go back to being a highhanded dick. That Davis was easier to deal with.

"Will it be safe for us to leave?"

"You'll always be safe with me."

That sounded a lot like a promise and hearing it spoken softly made it harder to remember it was his job to keep me safe. Though, I wasn't paying him to do this particular job and I was too afraid to ask if Trevor was paying Takeback. Sometimes ignorance was bliss. If Trevor was paying I'd have to walk away from Davis and as much as I talked a big game about taking on my father alone, the truth was, he scared the hell out of me. The thought of being taken back to Montana and being used as payment for whatever problem my father found himself in didn't terrify me—it made me wish for death.

"So there are times my safety's negotiable," I teased in an effort to lighten the mood.

Davis read my tone and dropped his hand but didn't move.

"Did you miss the part about being safe with me?"

I wasn't sure that was true.

Being alone with Davis was the exact opposite of safe.

"Davis…" I started then stalled because I wasn't sure what I was going to say.

He stepped back while at the same time pulling his phone out of his pocket.

"Just go with it," he muttered.

Just go with it…

That sounded dangerous…to my heart.

CHAPTER NINE

Jane walked out of the bathroom, the sight before me so fucking gorgeous I had to look back down at the linen shirt I was buttoning before I rushed her and ripped the dress she was wearing clean off.

"Is this alright?" she asked.

I kept my gaze firmly diverted and answered, "Yup."

I let that hang and offered no more because the only thing I had beyond my short, one-word answer would have her rushing back into the bathroom, locking the door, and possibly calling the cops.

By the time I finished with my shirt she was standing next to me. The scent of orchids and pineapples hit me. She looked hot as fuck and smelled good enough to eat. Which was exactly what I was going to do if we didn't get out of this room and go downstairs to get married.

"Davis?"

"Yeah?" I returned without looking at her.

"You don't have to do this."

Hell no, we weren't having this argument again. It was settled or I thought it had been.

"We're doing this," I told her and grabbed my tie off the dresser in front of me.

"You seem…"

Jane paused and didn't go on.

It was then I made the mistake of lifting my head. The moment I did I wished I hadn't. Pretty green eyes full of worry stared back at me. Her bottom lip was captured by her teeth and the urge to kiss the worry away overwhelmed me.

"I seem, what?" I stupidly asked, knowing I didn't want to hear her answer and delay leaving.

"Angry? Mad? Unhappy?" she rapped out and concluded on, "Different."

In less than twenty minutes I was marrying a beautiful woman, who was the sister of my sworn enemy, and all I wanted to do was tear the flowy white dress from her body, bury my face between her legs, and see if she tasted as good as she smelled.

Was I angry? No.

Was I unhappy? Fuck yeah.

"I'm fine."

"If you say so," she muttered disbelievingly.

I reached beyond the tie I decided not to wear and nabbed the ring box.

"Ready?"

Jane's gaze cut to the tie.

"You're not going to wear it?"

Fuck.

"Do you want me to?"

Her eyes cut to my chest and she shook her head. Then without warning her hands lifted to the collar of my shirt. The feel of her hands working the top button had me fighting against my body's reaction to her touch.

Fuck.

We had to get out of this room.

"If you're not going to wear it you need to undo a few buttons."

Her hands slowed, her gaze cut to mine, then suddenly she stepped back, losing purchase on my shirt.

"I'm sorry," she blurted. "So sorry. I shouldn't have touched you without asking."

Fuck.

She had it all wrong.

My hand shot out, tagged her wrist, and yanked her back. Her free hand went to my chest to stop herself from crashing into me.

"You look amazing," I told her and watched her eyes flare. "So, to circle back, I'm not angry, I haven't changed my mind about getting married. I'm trying really fucking hard not to tear the pretty dress off and give you sex hair in our official wedding picture."

Those green eyes were no longer full of worry. They were full of hunger, a look on her that was such a turn-on, I lost the fight against going hard—something Jane didn't miss. But she didn't pull away.

"Davis—"

"We need to leave this room, go downstairs, and get married. After that we'll come back up here, grab our shit, and head out. After that we'll find someplace to go to dinner."

"Davis—"

"Baby, do me a favor and get your sweet ass to the door, yeah?"

She didn't move her sweet, round ass. Instead she gave me a squinty, pissed-off look that did nothing to calm my reaction to her.

"*Honey,* do me a favor and stop interrupting me," she snapped.

Damn, she was feisty. Which made me wonder if I'd been attracted to the wrong kind of woman all this time or if it was just her attitude that made my blood burn and my dick hard.

"Maybe I didn't make myself clear when I said we need to leave."

"Oh, you've made yourself crystal clear," she said and brushed her hip against my erection. However, she still didn't take pity on me and head for the door. Though she lost her attitude when she softly said, "Before we leave I just wanted to say thank you. I know I haven't made it easy and I've pretty much been an argumentative bitch since you found me but I do appreciate everything you're doing. Including saving me from myself and not letting me pull my normal stubbornness. So, again, thank you."

Goddamn, she was making it seriously difficult not to kiss the living hell out of her.

We needed to get out of this room...now.

"You're welcome, Jane."

"And thank you for saying I look amazing," she shyly whispered.

Well, that answered that.

It was Jane.

Shy, bold, confrontational, stubborn, full of vim and vigor, or scared.

The woman could run the gamut of emotions in the space of an hour, all the sides of her appealing. Except when she was scared and trembling. That wasn't appealing, yet it was, only because I got the sense she didn't allow herself to be vulnerable in front of anyone. And if I'd have to guess that included her brother. So in a twisted, fucked-up way, giving me her fear attracted me to her more than all the other sides she'd shown me.

"Now I'm ready," she finished and removed her hand from my chest.

I immediately felt the loss of her touch and that made me seriously unhappy knowing the next time I got it we would be in front of an officiant performing our fake wedding.

The vows would be fake.

The kiss at the end would not be.

———

"YOU MAY KISS YOUR BRIDE," a young, brown-haired woman declared.

I didn't hesitate.

I moved in and the kiss was not only not fake but far too indecent for public. I didn't give the first fuck. I also didn't stop until Jane moaned, indicating it was time to break the kiss before lewd turned into vulgar.

That was a mistake and I contemplated going in for another kiss just to erase the soft look and fluttering of Jane's lashes as she opened her eyes.

Fuck me.

"Jane?"

"Huh?"

"Babe?"

"Yeah?"

Christ, she was killing me.

"You can let go."

Her hands slid out of my hair where she'd claimed purchase during our kiss and she jumped back. It was cute. It was hot. She looked to be in a daze and as much as I liked that I needed her to snap out of it before the tightness in my pants became visible.

"Congratulations, Mr. and Mrs. Wright. I've already signed your marriage certificate. It's waiting for you at the front desk. Enjoy the rest of your day."

I vaguely wondered how Wilson pulled off a fake certificate

so fast. Likely he'd called Shepherd, a computer guy we used from time to time if what we were looking for went beyond what Rhode could find. Wilson also used Shep when what we needed was behind some serious layers of protection, meaning the hack wasn't just illegal it was seriously fucking illegal and he wanted to keep Rhode clean.

Jane thanked the officiant, I gave her a dip of my chin, then tagged my wife's hand. It wasn't until after I picked up our certificate and we were waiting for the elevator doors to open that I felt the sharpness of her ring between my fingers. A delayed reaction since it had taken that long to get the taste of her—not to mention the hazy gaze she'd given me—from my mind. Now the weight of the ring she'd slid onto my finger sat there at the base of my finger. A heaviness that couldn't be measured in grams or ounces but in duty.

The marriage was fake.

But my vow to keeping Jane safe was a commitment I wouldn't fail at. And if that took months or years to accomplish, I was all-in. I had a feeling she was not. She'd want a divorce as soon as she felt safe enough to do it. Evidence was suggesting I'd burn any such papers.

Seeing as she was who she was, the thought was ridiculous. But it was no less true. Jane Morgan—no, Jane Wright—was not the sister of Zeus, she was Jane.

Complicated, complex, outspoken, sweet, shy-at-times, Jane.

Multifaceted.

Like the diamond I'd given her.

Strong and unbreakable.

Dazzling and beautiful.

"WELP." Jane popped the P and glanced around the small one-room beach shack that the man at the marina had called a cabana. "This isn't the Four Seasons."

If the smile she sported while looking around was any indication her statement wasn't a jab at our new accommodations but relief.

"You good with staying here?"

"Oh, yeah."

And there it was, confirmation she felt more comfortable in a shack than luxury.

"This place is rad," she went on.

I took in the sparse furnishings, all wicker, all worn and well-used. The small bed in the corner that couldn't be a queen but was bigger than a single. The kitchenette that had the smallest fridge I'd ever seen that wasn't one of those under-the-counter mini fridges. It was aging yellow, chipped, but by the sound of the thing humming I'd guess it cooled. The stove wasn't any better than the fridge and the countertops were old and discolored.

In other words, the shack was not rad. It was total shit. It was also a place that back in the day my mother would've loved and she'd likely still love. The only vacation she'd ever taken me on was to a cabin. It looked a lot like this place only in the mountains feet away from a stream instead of the ocean. The days we spent in that cabin was the only time I could remember her being truly happy. Out in nature with her boy, far away from all the problems she had back in the city. My mom hadn't called the cabin rad, she'd called it heaven.

My mother no longer lived paycheck to paycheck. She no longer had to eat whatever food I hadn't finished at dinner. She no longer looked skinny and unhealthy. As soon as I could I set her up in a condo on a golf course with a small backyard because she wanted a garden. I would've set her up in a mansion, but she wanted low maintenance and a clubhouse so that was what she got even though I wanted to see my mom set up in a palace.

"What are you thinking about?" Jane asked softly.

"My mom. She'd love it here."

I didn't miss Jane's shock I'd answered honestly. Hell, the yesterday me would've blown her question off totally.

"Does she live in Idaho?"

Her question was tentative. Interested but not prying.

"No, she's still in Phoenix. When we moved Takeback's headquarters to Idaho, I asked her to move north with me but she refused. She not only has a huge circle of friends but she's one of those weird people that loves the valley because it's hotter than Satan's taint, not despite it."

Fuck.

"I'm—"

Jane quickly cut me off with a wave of her hand followed by, "You can make Satan jokes, Davis. Hearing his name doesn't bother me."

That was good to know but it bothered the fuck out of me.

"So she still lives in Phoenix," she smoothly guided the conversation.

"Yup."

"Has she visited Idaho?"

"After a month's worth of research she deemed the weather in Idaho acceptable in August. She came for a week and loved it. But she loved going home to Arizona where it was twenty degrees hotter than Coeur d'Alene and that was during the hottest part of the summer."

Jane smiled and noted, "Of course she loves it. There's a lot to love."

Now was the perfect time to ask something that had been bugging me since she'd told me that people treated her like shit growing up.

"Is that why you stayed in CDA?"

Her gaze darted around the shack. Not dodgy, not elusive, just contemplative.

Shit. Maybe we should be sitting for this conversation instead of standing in the middle of the room.

"I went down south to Moscow for college. It's beautiful down there but I was homesick. I grew up in Coeur d'Alene. As shitty as people treated me, I couldn't stay away. I wanted to go home. And by then my father had moved his club to Montana so I felt safe to go home. And…" she trailed off and looked uncertain.

"And, Zeus was there," I finished for her.

"*Trevor* was there," she corrected.

I clenched my jaw in an effort to not remind her Trevor and Zeus were the same person.

It was like she read my mind when she went on, "I know you can't differentiate the two. To you they're the same person. But to me, Trevor is my brother. Zeus is the MC president I want nothing to do with. Unfortunately, you're right and they're the same person so I can't have my brother the way a sister should. But, yes, he was back in CDA and I hoped that I could make him see what he was doing wasn't winning some stupid war he'd waged against our father. He was proving everyone right—he wasn't any better than Satan. He'd become what everyone said he'd be. But it was too late. He'd chosen his path and he was too far gone to save."

"But you stayed."

She shrugged and mumbled, "It's home."

"Harley Jenkins?" I asked about one of her many identities.

"Trevor's idea. When I moved back he showed up at my apartment and gave me a new identity. At first I thought he was trying to protect me by giving me a new name but I quickly figured out Trevor no longer did anything that didn't directly benefit him so my guess is he gave me a new name to put distance between us so his enemies couldn't use me against him. As small as CDA is, it's not *that* small, and by then it had grown from what it was when I was a kid. A lot of transplants from other states had moved there. A lot of people I'd gone to school with had left. Sure, some people knew who I was and the connection, but mostly by then they left me alone when they saw I was trying to move on, and part of that was when they learned I'd changed my name, even if it was Trevor's doing. I didn't correct the assumptions, mostly because I had moved on from being a biker's daughter and I didn't want to add biker's sister to that."

"Jane Morgan?"

"I didn't like the name Harley. It's not that it's a bad name, it's actually cool, but Trevor gave it to me and the more I learned about what he was doing I didn't want anything from him, especially something as important as my name. So I picked a name that fit and Jane was born."

Jane had refused to stay in a hotel that her brother had paid for. I could totally see her not wanting to use the name her brother had given her either.

But Jane.

"How does the name fit you?"

Her eyes went to the bed and stayed there when she answered, "You know, Plain Jane. Jane Doe. Take your pick, they're both me. I'm a no one, unidentified, faceless. And I don't mind being that. I prefer being that. Being someone or meaning something to someone means you have to share. Sharing leads to people knowing you. And the one and only good lesson Trevor taught me is people are dangerous and should be avoided."

There was a lot to unpack there. Jane was nowhere near plain. She was gorgeous, and from what I was learning, that beauty went beyond her outward appearance. But that wasn't the part that bothered me.

"You're not no one."

"I am, and as I said, I prefer it that way. Anonymity is my friend. I keep to myself. I don't have friends. I don't have relationships of any kind, and when they start to form I make sure to cut ties and remove myself from the situation as fast as I can."

I read and reread the file that Rhode had put together on her. That, coupled with Shep's intel, confirmed what she was saying. They found no friends, no boyfriends, no roommates, nothing on her credit cards or in her bank account that showed her going out to bars, going to concerts, sporting events, skiing, vacations, nothing. She kept to herself and now I knew why. That knowledge burned.

"That's why you change jobs so frequently," I surmised.

She nodded.

"You've been at the fence company for a while."

My wife gave me a sad smile I'd give the entirety of retirement—and that fund was healthy and would allow me to live out my life not having to worry about money even if I wanted to spend it frivolously—to never see that look on her beautiful face again.

"I'm the only one in the office," she explained. "The guys all work out on jobsites and I'm both the receptionist and the bookkeeper. My boss comes and goes from the office but he's a man and by that I mean he'd no sooner instigate small talk than pry into my personal life. He comes in, gets what he needs, grunts his appreciation and leaves. Every few months he gives me a small raise and I think he does that because I don't bring drama or bad moods to his office. I don't call in sick because I went out the night before and tied one on so I'm too hungover to go to work and I don't take personal calls because I don't have anyone in my life who would call me."

I believed her boss appreciated all of that but no boss would give out a raise every few months based on that alone, which meant she was also good at her job. But in the future she was going to be calling in sick because she went out the night before and tied one on. She was also going to be taking personal days because she'd be going down to Phoenix to meet my mother. And she'd take more because North Idaho had bomb-ass ski resorts and we were going to go as soon as it snowed. But before that I was taking her fishing out on the lake and maybe up to Rhode's cabin in Sandpoint. Not only was it a kickass cabin but there was shit cell service up there, and since that was the place he took Brooklyn and their son to disconnect from life and connect as a family, there was no internet.

Jane Wright would not live the same life Jane Morgan had.

Not while she was tied to me and my ring was on her finger.

I didn't tell her any of that.

Instead I gave her what I sensed she needed—a break from the heavy.

"As gorgeous as you look in that dress, why don't you change into something comfortable and we'll hit the beach before we head to the city and get dinner."

Her head tipped to the side and she studied me. I wasn't sure if she was ascertaining the veracity of my statement or if she didn't want to drive the twenty minutes to Lanai City. Either way I let her do it.

I learned it was neither.

"I'd rather go to the grocery store and cook here."

"We'll hit the store while we're there and stock up. But you're not cooking on your wedding night and I'm sure as fuck not cooking on mine."

Next I learned a valuable lesson about denying my wife.

"Davis," she murmured softly. "That's sweet but I'm kinda tired of eating out and I like to cook and haven't been able—"

"Get changed, we'll hit the beach for a bit, then head to a grocery store."

Jane smiled on a whispered, "Thanks, Davis."

That was to say, I couldn't deny her. And if that earned me her sweet smile I was fucked.

CHAPTER TEN

"Damn, Jane," Davis said around a mouthful. He chewed, swallowed, then finished, "You said you could cook, not that you served heaven on a plate."

That felt nice.

Too nice.

It was becoming harder and harder to remember who Davis was and why he was with me. From telling me he was trying not to give me sex hair before our wedding, to the kiss he gave me after we were pronounced husband and wife, to the way he let me off the hook when he noticed I was uncomfortable with our earlier conversation, to holding my hand as we walked around the small beach cove near the cabana, to smiling at me, teasing me, laughing like we were a real couple, to giving in about going out to dinner—all of it was too much. And before that he hadn't made me feel foolish for wanting to leave the hotel Trevor was paying for and he hadn't made a comment about our new accommodations, which were far from luxury or paradise but a place where I'd be comfortable.

So complimenting me on my cooking wasn't the first

compliment he'd given me today which was why it was getting hard to remember my place.

I was his fake wife.

Period.

"It's just fish tacos."

"No 'just' about your fish tacos, Jane."

He was being generous. There was only so much you could do with tilapia.

But he looked like he meant what he said.

"Thanks."

We lapsed into silence as we ate. This was not uncomfortable, it felt natural and easy. Normal, or it would be if we weren't sitting at a teeny-tiny table that had seen better days, pushed against the wall off the small kitchen, a table that was barely big enough for our plates and glasses. Those plates being paper and the glasses being red Solo cups. Mine filled with champagne, Davis's with beer after he'd had his champagne.

The champagne was Davis's idea. So was the toast he made that was simple and to the point but something I'd never forget. Because that toast would be the one and only toast I'd ever have on my wedding day since after we were divorced I planned on never getting married again.

I'd be lying if I tried to deny the thought of divorcing Davis knotted my stomach. It was because of that—the knot in my belly and the hurt in my heart—I broke the quiet.

"What did Wilson say about when we could go back to Idaho?"

Davis had stepped outside to speak to his boss while I was cooking dinner. I didn't question why he'd done this and I hadn't asked because I didn't want reality to creep back in. But that was stupid; I needed reality. I needed to remind myself that one day soon we'd leave this hideaway and go back to life.

"The photographer already sent him the pictures from

today. He picked one and sent it to the *Coeur d'Alene Press* to go with our announcement. He also sent the same to the *Valley Journal*. Not sure if your father or any of his brothers read the paper or go online to get local news but our announcement will be on the *Journal's* website by morning."

Satan read and watched the news religiously.

Shit.

This was happening. There was no going back now. Tomorrow my father would see I'd married a member of Takeback. Davis's plan would either work and my father would figure out I wasn't worth the trouble or it would piss him off to such an extreme he would scorch a path to Idaho and snatch me up himself.

Only time would tell.

"He's thinking at least a week. Maybe more. Maybe less if your father reaches out to your brother, something Zeus says he'll do when he sees the announcement."

He would.

My father would call Zeus and lay into him. He'd also blame Zeus for allowing me to marry an outsider. He'd do it ugly and my brother would deny that my father calling him to give him shit would cause him pain but it would.

How could it not?

Like it or not the man was our father—a horrible one, but still we were his blood.

Being nearly abducted had scared the hell out of me. Being stalked all the way to Hawaii, the same. But that order coming from my father made it worse. Knowing that the man who made me didn't care about me at all, had no love for me, not even common decency, killed even if I hated him. And by hate I meant I loathed him down to my bones. Yet I didn't want him stalked, abducted, and sold into a life of sex trafficking. Put in jail for the rest of his life, yes. Violated and terrified every day, no.

"He'll see the *Journal* and call Trevor tomorrow," I mumbled, staring at my unfinished dinner.

Perhaps I should've waited to have this conversation until after I was done eating. The fish tacos were really yummy and now they'd go to waste.

"Jane?"

"Yeah?"

"Baby, look at me."

It was the gentle 'baby' that had me lifting my gaze to meet his.

"Everything's going to be okay."

"Sure it will."

I didn't mean that snarky and I knew he read me right when Davis's whole face softened.

"You have to trust me. Trust my team. Trust that as fucked-up as your brother is, he's doing his part to protect you, too."

That almost made me smile.

"How hard was it for you to say that last part?"

"I'm still choking down the burn."

Davis said it teasingly but I knew he was telling the truth. And that burn was for me.

Oh, yeah, I could barely remember this whole thing was fake.

"Thanks," I whispered.

"Everything's going to be okay," he repeated.

This time my "Okay" was a little more convincing.

After dinner I found out my new husband did the dishes.

I also learned he liked reality TV.

"Please tell me you're not serious," I said when he stopped on the Discovery Channel.

"What? You don't like *NAKED AND AFRAID*?"

"Um…" I sputtered and my eyes went back to the television set that looked like it was purchased sometime in the '80s, grateful that high definition hadn't yet become a thing. "She's naked and digging into that dude's armpit. And seeing as she's picking something out of there that's most likely a flesh-eating bug I don't think it's a good idea they're sitting in muddy water."

Davis smiled.

I scrunched my nose and went on, "That's nasty."

"The naked part?"

"Are you *not* seeing the muddy water? There could be fish swimming around looking for something to eat. Soon the armpit bug might not be the only problem the dude has."

"So you're worried about his dick—"

"Becoming fish food," I quickly cut in. "It's just bobbing and floating under the water like a lure."

Davis busted out laughing.

I watched him and I did this with avid devotion. Everything about Davis transformed and I realized that all the times he'd laughed before weren't laughs as such, they were more like chuckles. Now he was fully committed to the act and it was beautiful. I wasn't sure how a man who looked and acted like Davis could be described as beautiful but there it was. In all his rugged good looks he was absolutely beautiful when he was carefree.

This did not help me remember who we were. Further, it didn't help when he hooked me around the shoulders and pulled me against his side. The worn-out, beat-up wicker couch was already small enough that our legs were touching, I didn't need to be any closer. Apparently Davis was of a different mind when he held me close. Not knowing what to do with my hand, I opted to rest it on his chest.

"Thanks again for dinner," he said and settled in to watch his show.

"It was just—"

He gave me a squeeze. I shut my mouth, or at least I did for a moment before I started again, "My pleasure."

"Now, you good watching this or do you want to channel surf and find something else?"

I had a feeling he could scan all the channels cable had to offer and I still wouldn't find a show I could focus on while I was laid up against Davis.

I didn't tell him that.

"Sure, but if the guy's penis gets bitten off I get to say I told you so."

This time when Davis busted out laughing I didn't get to watch, but I felt his big body shaking under mine and that was better…way freaking better.

The next thing I knew I was floating. Not floating so much as being lifted, but in my semi-awake, mostly-out-of-it-because-I'd-been-asleep state it felt a lot like floating. Not floating as in soft, fluffy clouds—because there was nothing soft about Davis —but floating in the warmth and strong arms of a man who I knew would keep me safe.

I was in deep.

Too deep.

But luckily I was only semi-awake, mostly out of it because this meant I couldn't freak out. Nope, I couldn't freak out about Davis carrying me the five steps it took him to place me in bed, and not about that bed being the only one in the cabana, and not when he softly asked, "Wanna change, baby?"

I must've answered in the negative because he got into that one-and-only bed with me, rolled me to my side, and cuddled in.

Cuddled. In.

Big spoon, little spoon. With me being the little spoon, him the big, and when he draped his arm around me and held me close I was too out of it to do anything but snuggle back and soak him in.

I felt his hand find mine, his thumb brushed over my wedding ring, and my eyes shot open.

It was dark. Or as dark as it could be with the moonlight streaming in through the sheer curtains.

I was no longer in a semi-awake-but-groggy state. No, I was wide awake and fighting all of the freakouts I should've had already but didn't because I'd been lost in a dream that I never knew I could dream—being in the arms of a good, clean man who would keep me safe.

"Relax and go back to sleep," Davis mumbled against the top of my head.

That wasn't going to happen.

I sucked in a breath in preparation to tell him just that but all the air whooshed out before I could say a word.

"I got you, Jane. Just sleep, baby."

I closed my eyes as tightly as I could, pinched my lips together so I wouldn't embarrass myself by saying something like *please never, ever leave me*, and willed sleep to take me under.

It didn't. Not for a long time.

But there in the silence, in the dark, with Davis wrapped around me I started to wonder if Trevor was wrong.

Wrong about people using what they knew about you to manipulate you.

Wrong about never trusting anyone.

Wrong about never getting close to anyone.

Just *wrong*.

Because if this was what trust felt like I'd been missing out.

Ditto on the closeness.

I was slowly drifting off when I heard Davis whisper, "That's it, baby, sleep."

And I slept.

THE NEXT MORNING I woke up alone.

I wasn't sure if I was relieved or disappointed.

Nope.

That was a lie.

I was totally disappointed and that was dangerous.

Last night I'd fallen asleep leaning against Davis before *NAKED AND AFRAID* was over. Side note: the dude's penis hadn't become fish food but he did have ticks. *Blah!* I'd closed my eyes to ward off the disgustingness and didn't reopen them until I felt Davis fiddling with my ring.

And what was up with that? It was sweet. It was gentle. It was something a new husband would do with his real wife. Not a fake husband with a woman he barely knew.

I heard a door slam and I looked in that direction just as Davis stepped in from the rickety porch facing the beach. The door was a screen door without the intent of keeping the bugs out. Or, if it was meant for that, it failed due to the holes and tears in the screens.

"Coffee's ready," Davis said as he made his way into the kitchen.

I glanced at the mug he was carrying and wondered how long he'd been awake. Or better yet what time it was. Yesterday I'd noted there wasn't a single clock in the cabana. I didn't know if that was an "island time" thing or if the cabana didn't see many overnight guests so the owner didn't bother with clocks.

"What time is it?"

"Just past ten."

Ten.

Holy shit.

I'd slept for at least nine hours.

I couldn't remember the last time I'd slept that much in a twenty-four-hour period. I knew I hadn't slept that long since my father's asshole-lackey paid me a visit and before that I averaged six hours tops.

I rolled to the edge of the bed—more like a scoot than a

full roll—and tossed my legs over the edge while asking, "Why didn't you wake me?"

Davis was mid-pour when he asked, "Wake you?"

"Yeah. Why didn't you wake me up when you got up?"

His gaze was steady on me but at my question his eyes started to roam—my face, my hair, then back to holding my stare.

"Baby, you need your sleep."

Again with the *baby*.

Hearing him call me that was the sweetest torture and it was going to send me straight to hell when I stopped getting it.

I should've told him to stop calling me sweet names and call me Jane.

I didn't do that.

"Nine hours is a little excessive."

"More like fourteen."

"What?"

"It wasn't even eight when you passed out."

That was impossible.

Though it was semi-light outside when we started watching TV and we hadn't taken a year at the grocery store and fish tacos were easy and quick.

But eight.

I hadn't gone to sleep at eight since I was…well, eight.

Davis brought his mug up to his mouth, which brought my attention to his lips, and right then they were tipped up and he was grinning.

"Why are you smiling?"

"Because you're cute when you're confused."

"I'm not confused," I semi-lied because I wasn't totally confused—just confounded that I'd slept hard and long and felt more rested than I had in months.

"Being on the run takes it out of you," he sagely noted.

I said nothing to that because he was right and obviously he knew that since he'd said it.

"You want coffee?"

"Am I breathing?"

I heard Davis chuckle and watched him open the cabinet above the coffee machine.

"On a scale of grow hair on your chest and watered down how strong is the coffee?" I asked as he poured the nectar of the gods into the fresh mug.

"Two steps down from hair on your chest."

"You're perfect," I breathed. Davis's gaze sliced across the room and bore into me. I rushed to correct myself. "I meant, *that's* perfect."

"Right."

He elongated the word.

Shit.

"I'll wait for you out on the porch."

I watched Davis walk to the door, kick the bottom wood portion, and walk out with my coffee.

I might've moaned at the delay of my morning brew.

Or maybe it was because Davis had on loose-fitting workout shorts that highlighted his perfect ass.

"I heard that!" he shouted.

"You stole my coffee."

"Then get your ass out here."

I hopped up and got my ass out there, telling myself it was because I wanted my coffee, not because I wanted to sit next to Davis on the porch looking out over the beach while I enjoyed my morning coffee.

Hey, sometimes a girl's gotta do what she's gotta do to get through the day.

CHAPTER ELEVEN

The moment Jane's ass hit the padded seat of the patio chair she twisted to the small table that was between us and picked up her coffee.

"I take it you like coffee?"

"Live for it," she muttered, cradling the mug with both hands. She brought it to her mouth.

"Forgot to ask you how you take it."

She took a sip, lowered the mug a fraction, and said, "Any way it comes as long as it's strong."

That was unusual. People typically liked their coffee how they liked it and only how they liked it.

"Seriously?"

She nodded then added, "Sometimes I'm in the mood for sweet or flavored or a latte. I like coffee in all forms. And I don't limit my coffee intake to the morning though that's a must or I can't start my day. Sometimes I like a cup midday or after dinner. Again, I just like it. Some people like soda or tea. I like coffee." When she was done her gaze dropped to my mug and noted, "No creamer. Do you like sugar?"

"Nope. Black."

She nodded again like she was filing that away. Then she looked out to the ocean.

"It sure is beautiful," she mumbled her understatement. "Peaceful."

She wasn't wrong.

Other than a few charters that had gone out earlier, the marina had been mostly quiet. The beach was empty and other than a lone fisherman trolling back and forth no one else was out in the water.

"Why isn't that boat tied to the dock? Did it get loose?" Before I could turn to look, Jane leaned forward and went on, "Is someone…"

She didn't finish.

Or she did, by slamming her mug down on the table. I turned to see what made her shove herself to her feet.

"Davis!" she unnecessarily shouted since I was less than a foot from her and took off running toward the water.

No, not the water, the dock.

I was up chasing her when I finally saw what had her sprinting—there was someone in the water not far from the boat. I only caught sight of a head before it went back under.

Fuck.

I quickened my pace and ran past her. I was on the dock nearing the end when I heard Jane yell, "The sign on the office says closed."

That would be because the owner of the marina had closed the office when he left on the second charter.

I hit the water, popped up, and heard a splash behind me.

Fucking crazy woman.

Thankfully the boat was only a hundred yards off the dock. Unfortunately I didn't know how strong of a swimmer my new bride was.

I shifted to a sidestroke and yelled back to Jane, "Please tell me you can swim!"

"Swim team. Came in fifth in state. Breast and freestyle."

Well, fuck me running.

With the assurance this wasn't going to be a double rescue I dove back under the water so I didn't have to fight the current and quickly made my way to the boat.

My hand hit something solid. I opened my eyes, fought the burn, and saw a man tangled in a net.

Shit.

I wrapped my arms around the man's middle and kicked to the surface, but could only get his head above the water.

"What's—"

"Climb in the boat," I cut Jane off. "Find a knife. He's tangled."

I watched Jane take a few more strokes, then reach up and grab the side of the boat. She was struggling to haul herself over the side when I went back to the man. I felt for a pulse. Finding it pounding, I told him, "Just hold tight."

"I…" the guy stopped, coughed, then tried again, "I can't…"

"It's all good," I told him. "Just relax."

"Found one," Jane said.

Thank fuck.

Jane jumped back into the water. I felt a tug on the net. The more she pulled the harder it was to keep the man above the water.

"Prepare to hold your breath," I warned.

Jane popped back up, took in a huge breath, and dipped back under the water.

I counted to forty-five, expecting her to pop back again. I got to fifty and started to get worried. By sixty I was ready to take the guy back under with me to check on Jane when I felt the net give way. Five seconds later I had the guy free and was ready to dive under when Jane surfaced and immediately turned on her back and gulped for air.

Christ.

Fuck.

"Jane—"

"I'm fine." Cough. "Good." Cough. "Just…fine."

I couldn't think about the overwhelming relief that washed over me.

"What's your name?" I asked the man in my arms.

"Noah."

"Alright, Noah, we're gonna head back to shore. All I need you to do is relax."

"I think I can swim."

"Just float," I told him. "Relax and float."

Once Noah's body relaxed I looked over at Jane.

"You good to start back or do you want to rest a minute?"

"Ready."

Damn if she didn't sound ready.

"Okay, then nice and slow back."

We were halfway back to shore when Noah took a big breath and sounded strong when he said, "Thanks."

"Happy to help."

"Want me to do the rest of the way?" Jane offered.

Hearing that something loosened in my chest. A tightness I hadn't noticed.

Jane was fine.

Noah was fine.

It was all good.

"No, baby, I've got him."

Twenty feet from the shore I could stand, so I did. Noah did, too. Then Jane. And when she did the light-pink t-shirt she'd fallen asleep in last night, slept in, and hadn't changed out of clung to her curves. My gaze dropped to her chest, and now was not the time, but seeing her nipples clearly outlined under the wet fabric I felt my body start to respond.

"Jane, go on up to the cabana and get changed."

"But—"

"Baby." My eyes dropped back to her chest, this time not hiding I was checking out her tits in the hope she'd catch my drift. "Go change, yeah?"

It took a beat but I knew she got it when she crossed her arms over her chest and nodded.

"Yeah. Right. Okay. Glad you're okay, Noah."

Jane turned and was trudging through the gentle waves rolling in when Noah finally pulled it together and shouted at her back, "Thanks!"

Drama over, I finally took Noah in. My guess, he was in his twenties. Tall, thin, built as a twenty-something would be who worked on the water and likely surfed. He also resembled the man who owned the marina.

"Your dad own the place?"

"Yeah," he answered and looked to the left toward the office. This proved he was a good kid. He didn't watch Jane's ass in wet jean shorts as she maneuvered her way to the beach. Instead he stared at me.

Residual fear lingered but mostly all I saw was gratitude.

"Seriously, man, thanks for saving me."

"Glad we were out on the porch and saw."

Noah shook his head.

"I don't know how it happened. My net got caught, I jumped in, then I got caught. I've freed that net hundreds of times. Don't know how it happened this time."

With his dad owning the marina, this being Hawaii, I didn't doubt he'd been out hundreds of times with no incident.

Still…

"That's why it's called an accident."

"I guess," he mumbled miserably then shifted his attention back to the water.

"You need help getting your boat?"

"Nah. I got it."

"Right. Let me rephrase. Let's go get your boat and bring it in."

"You've done—"

I didn't let him finish.

"We grabbing a skiff or are we swimming out?"

The rest of the fear slipped out of his eyes and he smiled.

"Skiff."

I figured that would be his answer. I didn't know exactly how long he'd been out there treading water, getting pulled back down by that heavy net, but I knew from experience that shit was exhausting.

By the time we got Noah's boat, got back, tied it up, and I made sure he was good to be alone until his dad got back from the charter—which he told me was due back within the hour—Jane was freshly showered and sitting on the porch.

I took in the new loose-fitting, low-cut V-neck white dress with a big, light-blue leaves pattern. Even with her sitting I could see it cinched at her waist and landed mid-thigh. A dress that would give me easy access. A dress I would have bunched around her waist if we were a different kind of married.

She looked sexy as hell sitting there freshly showered, face openly beaming with happiness, eyes steady on me as I made my way to her.

"How's…" Jane stalled when I didn't slow my approach. "Davis?"

Her voice was nothing but a shaky breath when I bent down, planted my hands on the back of her chair, and took her mouth.

The kiss was unlike the others. It was slow and deliberate and lasted a long fucking time. But by the time I pulled back, I knew my message was received.

We were taking the fake out of our fake relationship.

CHAPTER TWELVE

Vaguely I heard the ringing of a phone. Which meant Davis unfortunately broke the second-best kiss I'd ever received in my life. The kiss before that now ranked third but only because there could only be one best kiss. The kiss I was currently mourning the loss of slid into second place because the way Davis had stalked across the porch with his eyes pinning me in place was hot.

The best kiss was still the one he gave me after he promised to love, honor, and cherish me for the rest of his life. The vows were lies, the kiss was sublime.

"Jane?"

"Huh?"

"Baby, you have to let go."

Damn.

Right.

I slid my hands out of his wet hair trying to remember how they'd gotten there when I heard him chuckle.

"Not sure what I like more—the taste of you on my tongue, the way you hold on when I kiss you, or the way you look when I'm done."

Without thinking I asked, "How do I look?"

"The way a beautiful woman should look after she's been kissed."

That wasn't the first time he'd called me beautiful, but this time when he said it I believed him.

With that, he straightened and went into the house to answer his phone.

I heard the screen door slam after him.

I looked out at the ocean.

I didn't get to study it for long because I heard footfalls, then the screen door open. I glanced over at the door and watched Davis come back out holding my purse, though I wasn't paying attention to my handbag. His chest had my attention—*all of my attention*. His very bare, very muscular chest. I followed the light dusting of hair that narrowed as it reached his abdominals and became a trail leading to what I knew. Not that I had firsthand knowledge, though I'd felt the evidence of the promise of all the goodness that trail led to pressed against my belly.

Davis had gone into the house wearing a mostly dry, but still-damp shirt.

Now he was not.

And my first thought was I really wished I hadn't slept in so late because I wanted to know if he slept with a shirt on. And if he didn't, how early I'd need to wake up so I could study all those ridges and valleys before he woke.

"Babe?" he called, his voice laced with what sounded like humor.

"Huh?"

"Jane?"

"Yeah?"

I knew it was humor I'd heard when his body started shaking with it.

"You need CPR?"

I wasn't sure, but I was thinking the evidence suggested I might.

"You're… you have a…" I snapped my trap shut and fought against the need to cover my own damn mouth with my hand to keep from blurting out what a great chest he had.

"I'm what?"

"Nothing."

His phone started ringing again. No, my purse started ringing.

Oh, shit.

"Jane?" This time my name was laced with concern. "Your phone."

There was only one person who had that number.

My brother.

"That's Trevor," I told him.

"Okay."

Okay?

"No, not okay. That's Trevor."

My phone continued to ring.

Davis continued to hold my purse out in front of him.

"Are you going to…"

Too late, it stopped ringing.

I watched my purse land on the chair with a thud so I missed Davis walking the few feet he needed to stand in front of me. I didn't miss him crouch.

Oh, boy.

He was way too close. From a distance, albeit a scant one, but still…his naked chest nearly stole my breath. Up, close, and in my space the 'nearly' part got erased and I sucked in a breath.

This was dangerous.

"It fucks me to say this, but you need to answer your phone."

I blew out my breath and asked, "What?"

"Put the man's mind at ease and tell him you're all right."

I couldn't believe my ears.

Davis loathed my brother. Despised him. Not only that, but he and the men he worked with were actively trying to put him behind bars, and he wanted me to put my brother's mind at ease?

"I don't understand."

"Neither do I," he mumbled under his breath. "Again, it fucks me, baby, but he's your brother and he's worried. If shit was not extreme and you didn't have your father's asshole brother trying to snatch you, no way would I advise you to take a call from Zeus. But from what you've said, how he was with you, what he protected you from, that man is worried. You should let him know you're safe."

I was not going to think about how that made me feel. Not that he was the sort of man who could logically separate situations but that he'd heard me when I explained my feelings about my brother. Not only had he listened and heard, he understood. He wasn't judging my love for my brother.

But that was not why he wanted me to answer.

"Hasn't Wilson told him I'm safe?"

"He has. But it's not the same." Davis paused, something flashed over his face, something that looked unpleasant. "Shit's complicated between the two of you. From what I can tell, you have boundaries when it comes to him. Can't say I didn't wish those boundaries were such he didn't touch your life ever, but again, this is extreme. Saying that to say this; it's okay for you to answer."

And, yes, I was correct.

He didn't want me to answer to put my brother's mind at ease. He wanted me to answer because he thought I needed to or wanted to and I wasn't doing it because I was with him.

"In the last few months, I've spoken to Trevor more than I have in the last ten years combined," I told him. "That's to say there's been five phone calls made to him from that phone and as you know, one visit to the compound before I left. So what I'm saying is, he doesn't enter my life. He knows better. He steers clear. I know that's for me but also for him. He doesn't want me in his business, but more—he doesn't want me to see who he's become. Both of which I appreciate. But you're right, I need to call him back and tell him I'm alright or he'll call Wilson and that's not cool."

"You've spoken to him less than five times in ten years?"

Okay, so perhaps Davis hadn't paid attention and heard me when I told him my thoughts on my brother.

"When he heard I'd moved back up to Coeur d'Alene after I graduated college he called. I stupidly thought that me being close meant I could help guide him back to being who I remembered him being when I was growing up. Within the first thirty minutes he disabused me of this notion. Still, I was home, he was close, so I persevered. An hour later I realized my big brother was truly gone. A few years later he called and wanted to know how much I owed in student loans. I refused to tell him, he told me I was stupid. He could pay them off and I'd be debt free. I asked him if he was ready to give up the Horsemen and be my brother again. He hung up on me. The last call I got was maybe three years ago to tell me our dad's MC was going to a rally in Washington and word was they'd be driving through CDA to get there. He gave me the possible dates. I hung up on him. I've seen him out and about but we do not acknowledge each other. You were right to call them boundaries. Trevor knows mine and it's very rare he enters my life."

When I was done, Davis was staring at me.

"What?" I snapped. "Did you think I had weekly chats with my felonious brother so we could plan his—"

"Don't," Davis growled. "Don't go back there, thinking me asking a question means I'm being a dick. I'm not sure if I'm happy as fuck to know he's done his best to keep you safe from his bullshit by keeping his distance or I now think he's a bigger dumbfuck than I did before. And that's saying something because the man rents ass by the hour, runs drugs and guns, and doesn't shy away from blackmail."

My heart hurt knowing Davis told it true. My brother did do those things.

"Why would you think he's a bigger dumbfuck now?"

"Babe."

That was all he said.

"Is that an answer?"

Davis's elbows came off his knees, his hands went to the armrest of the chair, and he leaned in.

"He's got his sister close. The sister he put a lot of care and effort into keeping safe before he took off so he knows how precious she is. And what does he do? Gets deeper and deeper into shit instead of pulling himself out so he could give you something good and clean and healthy. That's what makes him a dumbfuck."

I didn't get a chance to respond to that. Not that I was sure how to respond to that before his phone rang in the cabana.

"*Fuck.* Be back."

Davis straightened and when he did I had a new point of fascination—his thighs. Big, strong tree trunk legs. I wanted to reach out and trace the muscles. Thankfully he turned, thus saving me from doing just that.

He knows how precious she is.

I'd never been precious to anyone.

Ever.

"Babe," Davis called from inside.

I assumed that "babe" meant come inside so I got to my feet, grabbed my fresh mug of coffee I'd only managed to drink half of (something I'd have to rectify, and quickly), snatched my purse off the chair, and headed inside.

Davis was leaning against the kitchen counter with his ankles crossed, sneakers and socks gone, chest still bare.

This was getting worse.

Last night, I'd slept in yesterday's clothes and fell asleep on the couch and he'd carried me to bed. I didn't know what Davis had slept in since he'd woken up before me and was out the door for coffee. Call me strange, that didn't feel intimate.

This?

Him standing bare-chested and barefoot seemed intimate. Like the veil had lifted. Like we'd gone from polite company to something different.

"Wilson," he mouthed.

I nodded and waited for him to say more.

"Yeah, busy morning," he said, then to me. "Baby, call your brother back. He's called Wilson twice."

Busy morning?

Was that what he called an ocean rescue, a busy morning? I called it something else—scary. Thankfully the situation had ended well, but only because Davis had kept his cool. If it had just been me out there I would've been freaking out. But Davis's calm demeanor gave me something I hadn't known I'd been missing my whole life. And it wasn't just with Noah and how he'd reacted in that situation, it was all of it.

I couldn't say Davis being in charge gave me peace but it did smooth the edges of my fear. No. Knowing that I had someone who would stand next to me and would do something as crazy as marry me to get me safe did more than smooth the edges—it gave me hope.

As it turned out I didn't have to call Trevor back. He called me. I couldn't fight the eye roll so I didn't, and when my gaze came back to Davis he was smiling.

Shirtless, barefoot, and smiling.

Yes, this felt intimate and dangerous. Because of that, I set my coffee down on the small dinette table and turned around while digging through my purse to find the pay-by-minute phone I'd picked up at Dollar General before leaving Idaho. I didn't answer until I was back out on the porch.

"I'm fine," I said by way of greeting.

"So I've heard." My brother's angry voice came at me through the phone.

This time I was able to control the eye roll but not my attitude.

"If you've heard then why are you calling?"

"Why am I calling?"

Now he sounded angry and annoyed.

I tried to remember a time when Trevor didn't sound angry or annoyed. Certainly it wasn't any time in the last ten years.

The sad truth was, I couldn't.

He'd been an angry child, an angry teenager, and became even angrier the older he got.

"That's what I asked, Trevor."

"Satan's got plans—"

"I believe my marriage vows swashed his plans," I cut in. "Wasn't that the whole point of me marrying Davis, so Dad wouldn't want me?"

My question was met with utter silence. This silence went on so long I pulled the phone away from my ear to make sure I hadn't lost service, or the battery hadn't died.

"Trevor?"

"Do you not like the asshole?"

I felt my spine stiffen and now I was getting angry.

"Don't call my husband an asshole," I snapped.

"Sis—"

"And do not call me sister, Trevor. I stopped being that a long time ago," I reminded him. "I'm fine. I'm safe. I'm good. So if that's all you wanted I'm hanging up."

"I don't like this," he growled.

The nerve.

"I'd ask you what it is you don't like if I cared. But I don't. And just to point out you lost the right to not like things I got going on in my life when you decided to turn into our father. Now, *Zeus*, I'm going—"

"*You* don't call me that," he snarled. "And that's what I don't like. This attitude you're throwing at me now that you think you got some dick at your back."

Anger was history.

I was enraged.

"Are you seriously threatening me?" I whispered.

I didn't get to hear Trevor's response. Not because my battery died or because I lost service. Nope, there was enough battery left when Davis appeared on the porch, stomped his way over to me, and snatched the phone out of my hand.

There was also enough power left when Davis matched my brother's angry tone and clipped, "You're done and I mean more than this conversation, motherfucker. I asked your sister to call you back so you would know we've got her and you could hear that directly from her. And what do I get…no, what does *she* get for the effort? You being a motherfucker. Now my woman's sitting with her back straight like she's been electrocuted while simultaneously looking like she's been sucker-punched."

There was a moment of silence before, "No, Zeus, *you* hear this. As of yesterday afternoon Jane Wright ceased to exist for you and your piece-of-shit father. She's gone to both of you in a way that she was not before. You do not ever enter her life. Your father doesn't enter her life."

Another pause. This one longer. Five seconds. I knew because I was counting. Counting the seconds trying to get my heart rate under control.

"You try that and the problems you already had with Take-back escalate. You're not the only one who doesn't have an issue breaking the law. But the difference between me and you is, I protect what's mine. Though I figure we're alike in the sense I won't lose a wink of sleep when I put you to ground."

With that Davis pulled the phone away from his ear, stabbed at the screen, then found the power button and turned it off.

"Your brother's an asshole."

"Um…"

What the hell just happened?

Davis pocketed my phone then like nothing unusual had happened—as in, oh, say him just calling me his woman and telling Trevor he protected what was his while at the same time inferring he'd lose no sleep after he killed my brother.

He casually noted, "You haven't had breakfast."

I blinked—rapidly.

Then my back relaxed and I bent forward to hold my stomach while I busted out laughing.

When I was done, Davis was staring at me.

Not like I was crazy, which I was beginning to think I was. Not like I was the sister of the man he hated and he'd just made that overly clear. Not like I was his fake wife whom he only married to keep safe.

Nope.

Davis Wright was staring at me like I was precious.

Okay, now, what in the world was that about?

CHAPTER THIRTEEN

"Damn, Jane," I said around a mouthful of chicken enchilada. "I thought your fish tacos were heaven but I was wrong. This is."

I was not blowing sunshine.

The woman could cook.

"Thanks."

It was a shy murmur.

Forty-eight hours in and already I could call it.

The "it" being Jane's responses to something I'd said.

She was confident and she was sure of herself if the topic was anything to do with her adult life. She was proud and showed it when I'd asked her about when she moved to Moscow to attend University of Idaho. She had no issues expressing her opinions about what she wanted for her future. That future being the same as her present; boring, friendless, and alone. It was only when I complimented her she became shy.

The mystery that was Jane Morgan had been solved.

There was no complicated relationship with her brother because there was no relationship. There were only complicated emotions from a sister who loved the boy who had protected her but who hated the man he'd become.

She was not confident or sure of herself, though she thought she was and pretended to be because no woman who was self-assured got shy and borderline timid when someone reminded them of how great they were. They took the compliment in stride and didn't dip their heads to break eye contact. They stood proud in the knowledge that the other person recognized the accomplishment—big or small.

And lastly a woman who truly understood her worth wouldn't settle for a lonely existence. She wouldn't settle —*period*. She'd know down to her bones she deserved more and she'd fight to get it.

"May I ask you a question?" she asked, sitting opposite of me at the table yet not meeting my gaze.

As much as I wanted to tell her to look at me, I let it slide, but only because I knew she was feeling shy.

"Sure."

I took another bite and waited.

When she didn't speak, I looked up from my half-eaten enchilada and gave her my attention.

"Babe?"

"It's…ah…personal," she stammered and I smiled.

"I see you think I need that warning or maybe I have something to hide so you're giving me an out. But I don't, so just ask."

"It's about your dad."

Well, that explained why she was nervous.

"I don't have a dad."

"I mean—"

"I know what you meant," I cut in to save her from an unnecessary explanation. "And my answer's the same. I don't have a dad. My mother's husband knocked her up, stuck around for a few years, then decided a wife and son was not something he was interested in having so he took off."

I went back to my dinner thinking that would be the end of it.

"Sorry," she muttered.

"Nothing to be sorry for. I'm not dodging your question. There's just nothing to say. My mother has an ex-husband who didn't pay a dime of child support or alimony though he'd been ordered to do both since up until he left she was a stay-at-home mom. To avoid paying those I can only assume he either worked under the table, which I find unlikely since he was an accountant when he was married to my mom and made good money so he'd want to keep doing that, or bought a fake social and worked that way, or he died. Don't know, don't care beyond my mom had to work herself sick when I was a kid. I care a fuck of a lot about that. But she's good now and that asshole's been a ghost for over forty years so there's no sense in giving him headspace he doesn't deserve."

"It's that easy for you?"

"Is what that easy?"

"Not giving your dad headspace," she clarified.

"Baby, get this—I don't have a dad. I have no real memories of him. Don't know for a fact, I've never spent any time around three-year-olds, but my guess is, I wasn't even speaking in complete sentences when he bounced and left my mother—his *wife*. But even if he'd stuck around for longer and I remembered him I still wouldn't claim the man as my dad. A dad sticks. A dad teaches his child. A dad loves his son. A dad provides for his son. The asshole who had a part in making me bailed on his child and his wife. He's no father, certainly not a dad, and he's not the kind of man I want to know. So, no, it's not that easy. It is what it is and I have more important things to give my time and energy to."

Jane used the prongs of her fork to push around the bits of chicken left on her plate.

"I wish I could do that," she admitted.

I couldn't bring myself to explain to her the reasons why she couldn't. She hadn't moved past the hurt. She hadn't given up hope that Zeus would magically turn back into Trevor. Logically she knew her father was an evil motherfucker but her heart still longed for a dad.

"What did Trevor say to you today that set you off?" she asked.

I'd been waiting for her to ask and I was surprised it had taken all day for her to do it. I was also grateful because I didn't want to discuss her dickhead of a brother.

"Nothing worth repeating."

"He said he was going to tell my father our marriage was fake," she wrongly guessed.

That would've pissed me off.

Zeus telling me he was going to deliver Jane to their father personally didn't piss me off, it gave me an itchy trigger finger and burn-his-compound-to-ash vibes.

"No."

I got no more out when she guessed again.

"He said he'd take me to Montana and give me to Satan."

Fuck.

I contemplated lying but instead asked, "Why would you think that?"

"Because that's Trevor. When he's backed into a corner he loses his mind. When he feels like he's been disrespected he lashes out. And just so you know, you don't have to confirm I'm right because I know. You might not outright lie to me and I get that you think you're protecting me by being cagey but I know who Trevor is. I've always known that one day there was a chance he'd turn on me."

In an effort to contain the urge to find my phone and make

a call that would end Zeus's miserable life I went back to eating.

"Davis?"

I swallowed then said, "Need a minute, baby."

Apparently I needed more than a minute to get myself under control. The rest of my food was gone, though I didn't taste a single bite I took. Another reason to make the call, I'd missed out on the rest of heaven on a plate in the form of Jane's chicken enchiladas.

"He will not get to you," I told her.

"I know."

She knows?

Maybe she didn't understand the fullness of what I was saying.

I rested my elbows on the table and pinned her with a stare.

"He won't get anywhere near you. Neither will Satan. This is done for you."

"I don't know about done. I don't think it ever will be but I know neither of them will come near me as long as I'm married to you."

If I hadn't already been thinking of ways to convince her to stay married to me while I dated her and we explored what was going on between us, that would've done it.

My phone rang and I knew it was mine—even though earlier I learned that we had the same ringtone—because hers was in my backpack and turned off.

"I need to get that," I told her before I pushed away from the table. "Leave the dishes. I'll do them when I'm off the phone."

"I can—"

"Leave 'em, baby. You cook. I clean."

"Okay."

I tagged my phone off the coffee table, saw it was Wilson, and braced.

"Yo."

"We got a problem."

Fuck.

"A new one or did the old one escalate?"

"New, mixed with the old," Wilson said then went on to elaborate. "Brasco called. High school girl in Post Falls killed herself. Since the suicide was in Post Falls it's a different department. Brasco read about it in the paper, recognized the girl from the pictures Zeus is using as blackmail. He called the detective that caught the case. Found out the girl left a note. All it says is 'I'm sorry'."

"Fuck."

Zeus's latest attempt at proving he's a worthless asshole was to blackmail cops when he couldn't find any to buy off. So far he'd snagged three rookies using the same racket—underage girl in a bar who didn't look to be underage, had a fake ID, was already drinking in the bar so when she approached the cop he had no reason to think she wasn't at least twenty-one. Then when the cop took what was on offer the girl recorded the encounter and Zeus had the goods.

It was a fucked-up play but it was seriously whacked because the girls were not twenty-one, they were seventeen.

"Brasco's done waiting on IA to do their thing. Two of the cops are cooperating. The third is married and is playing dumb, willing to roll the dice and play Zeus's game in hopes whatever pictures he has don't get sent to his wife, who incidentally just gave birth. Brasco wants a meet with Butch."

Butch was a patched member of the Horsemen MC. He was also an undercover DEA agent who was at the end of his rope and getting frustrated. Butch had been the one to warn Takeback about the cops.

"He's not keen on meetups," I told Wilson, something he very well knew.

"A seventeen-year-old is dead. Brasco no longer cares who's keen on what. He's also not waiting for IA to finish their investigation even though he knows it's gonna fuck the cops who are working that angle of lying to Zeus, telling him he's covered when he's really not. And he really doesn't care that Stone Phillips is trying to save his marriage but fucking over the department in doing so. He's done, Davis, and he's pulled River in."

Fucking shit.

River Kent was Jet Brasco's partner. He was also married to Letty who was best friends with Brooklyn who was Rhode's fiancée. Further from that, River's siblings: Phoenix, Echo, and Shiloh were all cops back in Georgia. Meaning River's sense of justice was fine-tuned so he'd be all over fucking over IA to take down Zeus in light of a teenage girl taking her own life.

"They do that and the charges don't stick, he might fuck Butch."

"No shit," Wilson griped. "We all want this done but the DEA's been building their case for years. With that said, Zeus isn't their end game, he's a cog in a bigger game."

That was the first I'd heard of that. Not the years part—that was why Butch was at the end of his rope. He'd been breathing nothing but filth for a long time.

"Bigger game?"

"Bigger game," Wilson confirmed.

"Care to elaborate?"

"I would if I'd been fully briefed, which I haven't been. I've just been warned to keep Brasco in line."

That was a joke.

Jet Brasco was not a man you kept in line.

"I'm thinking the only line Brasco's willing to be kept in is maybe the gun section at Black Sheep."

"You're not lying. Got one more thing for you. Before Zeus's temper tantrum, and thanks for that by the way, now I have the asshole calling and threatening to nab both you and Jane."

My chest ignited and my throat clogged.

"Come again?"

"Ignore the dick like the rest of us are doing. You know damn good and well that stupid fuck doesn't have the balls to go after you or your woman."

It was good to know Wilson had picked up on that. Jane was mine, and that had nothing to do with the piece of paper I'd signed.

"Anyway," he continued. "Rhode got the announcement out and Zeus confirmed Satan has seen it. Called him this morning bright and early to ream his ass for allowing his sister to marry a pig."

I wasn't fond of cops being called pigs.

"Is that the cover Rhode put out? I was a cop before I worked for Takeback?"

"Nope. Your shiny new LinkedIn profile has your military career and Takeback as your current employer."

"So he's just an equal opportunity asshole."

"Yup. But he knows, he's not happy, and hit Zeus up for fifty K."

I heard the water turn on so I glanced over my shoulder and found Jane at the sink.

"Jane, honey, come sit down. I told you I'd do the dishes."

"I don't want to intrude, and since this place is one room, it's the kitchen or the bathroom and sorry, but I'm not sitting in that bathroom waiting you out."

"Come sit down, find something for us to watch. I'll wash while I finish talking to Wilson."

"Look at you all domesticated and shit," Wilson jabbered.

"I'd tell you to fuck off if that comment bothered me," I shot back, making my way to the kitchen.

"Huh?" Jane asked.

I pulled the dish out of her hand and said, "Nothing, baby. I was talking to Wilson."

"You tell your boss to fuck off?" she whispered.

I heard Wilson chuckle, meaning he heard Jane.

"Yeah, and I'm gonna tell him to fuck off again if he doesn't stop laughing."

Jane looked horrified. It was cute and so un-Jane-like I couldn't stop myself from leaning down and kissing her nose. "Go find something for us to watch, yeah?"

"Okay."

Soft and breathy.

I wasn't sure if I needed to keep Wilson on the phone for another ten minutes until I could get that sweet sound out of my head or if I needed to hang up now and find more ways to make her breathy and sweet. I knew what I wanted to do, but it was too soon.

"You're fucked." Wilson told me something I knew.

So I didn't bother denying it.

"Yup."

I picked up the sponge Jane had left in the sink and started scrubbing.

"What'd he say about the fifty K?" I asked, leaving Zeus's name out of the question.

"He paid it."

I nearly choked.

"Say that again."

"Zeus paid it. Fifty K for Jane's freedom."

Fury.

That was all I felt.

First, all Jane was worth to her father was fifty thousand.

Second, Zeus paid the debt—with dirty money.

She'd hate that.

No. She'd die a thousand painful deaths if she knew her freedom was bought from innocent people's misery.

"I need a favor."

Wilson sighed, long and loud.

"I already know what you're going to ask."

I bet he did. Wilson knew me well.

"There's forty in my safe at home. Float me the ten and I'll get it back to you when I get home."

"Davis—"

"She's *my* wife," I cut him off.

"On paper."

I had nothing to say to that because while that might have been true, Wilson also knew it wasn't. And if at the end of this she ended up being my ex-wife, it wouldn't matter.

I'd pay ten times that to ensure she was safe.

And I'd do that with hard-earned, clean money because that was damn well what she deserved.

"You know that's bullshit," I said.

Another sigh. This one not as long but just as loud.

"I hope to fuck you know what you're doing."

I had no clue.

"Let me know when it's done. And make sure he knows to keep his trap shut."

"Copy that."

Wilson disconnected.

I took my time washing dishes.

Fifty thousand dollars.

That was all Jane was worth to her piece-of-shit father.

The dumbfuck had no idea his girl was priceless.

CHAPTER FOURTEEN

Once again I woke up in yesterday's clothes.

Unlike yesterday I was not alone.

And unlike yesterday my cheek was resting on something hard and warm. My hand was resting there, too. I opened my eyes and saw what I'd feared...a dusting of hair covering Davis's chest. His bare chest, which answered yesterday's question—he slept shirtless. To make matters worse, I was mostly on my side, my leg thrown over his thighs, knee high near his groin.

Good Lord.

That wasn't all.

Davis's arm was around me and his hand was not resting on my bottom—he had a handful of mostly bare cheek. The mostly was because I had on a pair of panties that were not full bottom, but not G-string either. They were the cute kind that had enough material not to give you the all-day feeling that you had thread between your ass but not full-on granny panties.

So, yeah...

He had a handful.

But the absolute worst part was it had only taken seconds

for me to decide I wanted to wake to this or some variation of this for the rest of my life. I wanted to open my eyes in the morning and see Davis next to me. I wanted to feel his warm strength under me. I wanted it wrapped around me. I wanted to wake up next to a man who wouldn't hesitate to jump into the ocean to save a stranger's life, then go about his day like he hadn't saved a life. I wanted to know that whatever my day would bring, I'd come home to this—the knowledge that a good, clean man shared my bed. I wanted this to such an extreme it scared the hell out of me.

Since I knew I couldn't keep this, I lay there perfectly still, wanting to have it for as long as I could get it.

So that was what I did.

I kept perfectly still and thought back over yesterday. Day one of my fake honeymoon had started with a scary rescue and ended watching TV. The in between time had some really great parts—Davis asking me about the swim team, me telling him about it, then him telling me how 'amazing' he thought that was. He'd also gone on to tell me how impressed he'd been with how well I'd handled the situation with Noah. When I'd started to wave off his compliment he'd grabbed my hand, squeezed it, and said, "You are amazing, Jane." And the way he'd said it made me believe he meant it. We'd gone back to town, walked around some of the shops not needing anything and not buying anything. Just doing it for something to do.

It was the best day I'd ever had.

With no reason to hurry, no other place to be, we simply strolled. Conversation was light, teasing, and fun. Nothing heavy, which I sensed we both needed. When we got home I cooked.

The bad parts about yesterday—save Noah almost drowning, but Davis had saved him so really it ended up being good —all had to do with my brother. Not a surprise. I hadn't had a lot to do with Trevor in the last decade but I knew bad surrounded him daily. With Davis taking all of my attention, and in a way that felt good, I hadn't given Trevor much thought. But now in the early morning hours, with Davis's strength surrounding me I allowed my brother to do what I rarely allowed—I let him invade my thoughts.

I'd known going to him for help would open a door I didn't want open, but I'd had no choice. Now that the door was open it was clear Trevor was pushing his way through the crack and getting him back on the other side would get ugly—or uglier than it had been yesterday.

There was a reason Trevor got nasty when he felt himself backed into a corner—he'd had to fight his whole childhood to be seen, to be heard, to be respected, and to protect me. So, I knew it would get uglier and nastier because I'd seen it. I didn't think he'd actually follow through with his threat to deliver me to my father but the mere fact he'd said he would meant I needed to make a stand. Once and for all, I needed to cut the last string. The problem was I didn't know how to do that. The only string that was left was the blood relation we shared. Unfortunately I couldn't drain my Lawrence blood as easily as I'd changed my name.

"What has you concentrating so hard?"

Davis's gruff, morning voice pulled me from my thoughts.

No way in hell was I starting the morning discussing my brother. The other option would be telling him my previous thoughts and that was not going to happen either.

"How did Wilson know what size clothes I wear?"

Welp, that was lame but better than telling him I wanted to wake up next to him for the rest of my life.

Davis confirmed just how lame my statement was when I felt his big, hard, warm body start to shake. Then he cemented it with a chuckle.

"You're lying on me thinking about Wilson?"

"What? No! Well, sort of, but not really. I'm curious—"

"I'm teasing you, Jane."

I knew he was but still…

"I'm not thinking about another man." Then I took lame to a whole new level when I stupidly admitted, "Besides, I think you've ruined me for all other men."

Suddenly I was no longer wrapped around Davis. His hand no longer had a hold of my bottom. I was on my back with Davis looming over me. His blue eyes locked onto mine. He was so close I could clearly see the flecks of lighter blue that patterned his irises.

Wow.

"You think?"

"Um…I think what?"

"You *think* I've ruined you for all other men?"

Okay, so I knew he had.

But still I lied. "Ruined might be a strong word."

A smile tipped Davis's lips before he lowered his head, brushed his smile from my jaw all the way to my ear. He did this slowly and ever so lightly. And just as lightly he whispered, "No, Jane, *ruin* is precisely what I intend to do."

He couldn't've missed my shiver and if he had the moan that slipped out would've given me away. But the way his large frame stilled told me he didn't miss either.

"You on board for that?"

My body screamed *hell yes.*

My heart shouted *hell no.*

My body won when I nodded.

Davis rolled off me, grabbed my wrist, and tugged me back to my original position—cheek and hand resting on his chest.

This time it was my body that shouted *no.*

"I thought—"

"Not yet." His hand found mine and like the night before, he fiddled with my ring while explaining, "Cole and Mia went to your old place. She gave Wilson the sizes you wear."

Okay, so, I was still reeling from Davis telling me he was going to ruin me and really wanting to know what that meant for me physically. As in I really, *really* wanted to know, which meant right then I didn't care how Wilson knew what size clothes I wore, but still I asked, "Mia?"

"She works at Takeback. She's the one who answered the phone when you called. And I have to tell you, we were all there, including Wilson."

Davis paused, likely to give me a moment to digest what he'd said.

The afternoon I'd called, I was told Wilson wasn't in the office.

She'd lied to me.

Of course she had; I was the sister of the enemy.

"I'm telling you now because you need to know, but also shit like this tends to come out and when it does it can fuck things up. So I'm telling you now so I can explain. Yes, we were all there. But we were in the middle of something that required our attention. And yes, we needed to understand the nature of your call before Wilson spoke to you. That's not about you, it's about your brother and I think you can understand why we'd be cautious when it comes to him. Lastly, she asked you if you were in danger. You said no. If you'd told her the truth Wilson would've become available."

I closed my eyes wanting to block out the room. That did nothing to prevent me from feeling the warmth of his chest or the sweet way he was twisting my ring.

"I'm not mad. I get it."

"No, you don't. I know you think Mia not connecting you to Wilson was about you but it wasn't. And this is not a guilty by association thing. I'm telling you true, Jane, we were planning a takedown but if you'd admitted to Mia that you were in danger one of us would've gotten you safe."

I didn't believe that then but I believed it now.

"I know."

Davis's arm around me tightened. "Do you?"

"Now I do."

Davis's body relaxed, we lapsed into silence, and I thought it was safe to open my eyes.

I found I was incorrect. Now that the mystery of how Davis slept had been solved, and I knew how good it felt to be held by him, I needed to get up and out of this bed before I embarrassed myself.

"What else were you thinking about?"

"Nothing."

"I'll give you that play if you tell me what you're thinking about now."

Oh, boy.

"Davis—"

"Baby, you woke up with a jolt then went still and laid like that for a while."

"I did?"

"Did you have a bad dream?"

"I don't dream."

Davis stopped mid-twist of my ring.

"You don't dream?"

"No. At least I've never remembered any of my dreams."

"Never?"

Why was he being so weird about this? I couldn't be the only person in the world who didn't remember their dreams when they woke up.

"Never," I confirmed. "Maybe it's because I'm such a light sleeper and wake up multiple times in the middle of the night."

"You're a light sleeper?"

Now, I knew that wasn't strange. There were tons of over-the-counter medicines to help people sleep. Not that I took any of them but you can't watch TV or listen to the radio without hearing or seeing the commercials.

"Yeah."

"Jane, I've slept next to you two nights in a row. The first time I carried you to bed you woke up but last night you were out, didn't even open your eyes. I put you in bed, changed my clothes, locked up, and I wasn't overly quiet about that and you didn't wake up. Got in next to you, pulled you close, and the only thing you did was snuggle in. How is that light?"

As Davis spoke the muscles in my neck tightened. His words tumbled around in my head as I tried to make sense of what he was saying. Of course, it was the truth. He had carried me to bed last night and I hadn't woken up. I also had slept through both nights, not tossing and turning or waking up at any small noise.

That never happened, especially if I was in a strange place.

"Jane?" he whispered.

"I didn't wake up," I returned just as quietly.

Davis hummed but remained silent.

"Why didn't I wake up?"

His arm tightened around me but he didn't answer.

Or was that his answer?

Did I fall asleep on the couch with my head in his lap, stay asleep while he put me to bed, and not wake up through the night because Davis was there? Did I sleep soundly knowing Davis was in bed next to me?

"When I was little, Trevor would sleep next to me."

"You told me."

"I still woke up in the middle of the night. The slightest sound would wake me up."

Davis said nothing.

This lasted awhile as I tried to sort my head and it took a long time because I wanted to fight the truth—deny it, force it out of existence, pretend I didn't understand.

But I did.

I'd slept. I'd done it peacefully, I'd done it soundly, and there was only one explanation.

One reason.

One truth.

For the first time in my life I felt safe.

Totally safe.

At a time when I should've been up all night worried if my father would accept my marriage to Davis and leave me be, or if he was still after me, I'd slept like a baby.

I didn't get to tell any of this to Davis before he was sitting up, taking me with him, and suddenly on high alert.

"Get into the bathroom, baby," he said.

Then I was no longer in the bed because Davis was out of that bed standing next to it while setting me on my feet.

"Bathroom," he repeated and gave me a gentle shove.

The look on his face brooked no argument.

My feet took me to the small room as a knock came.

Davis stayed where he was until I shut the door.

Yes, safe.

Something I'd never been before.

A month ago a knock at the door would've scared the pants off me. Hell, a week ago I would've been trembling in fear. But now, mere feet away from potential danger with nothing but drywall and some flimsy paneling to protect me I'd never, ever felt safer in my life.

That was because it wasn't the drywall or the old, ugly paneling that would protect me.

It was Davis.

And I knew he'd do that bodily and he'd do it until I was safe or he wasn't breathing.

I didn't know how I knew that last part but I did.

That was the kind of man Davis was.

That was who he was for me.

He was the man I'd wished for my whole life but was told didn't exist.

Trevor was wrong—*again*.

I heard hushed voices, then a loud, "Jane."

There was no trepidation when I opened the bathroom door. I didn't wonder who was there, or what they wanted. If Davis was calling my name it was safe. Period.

As soon as Davis caught sight of me he launched in. "Baby, this is Kai, Noah's father. He's offered to take us out on the boat."

Oh, hell.

The last time I was on a boat—and that was on the still waters of Lake Coeur d'Alene—I was sick the whole time.

"Sure, that sounds great," I chirped.

Davis's beaming smile was worth the lie.

"THIS IS SO EMBARRASSING," I groaned.

Davis held the wet cloth on the back of my neck.

"Are you going to be sick again?"

Yes, again.

Again meaning he'd already held my hair while I puked.

Again meaning I was on my knees in front of the toilet.

Sexy, right?

"No."

"Wanna brush your teeth before I take you to bed?"

Gross.

"Umm, yeah."

Davis helped me to my feet, walked me to the basin, grabbed my toothbrush, and loaded it with paste. I watched him do this wishing I'd jumped off the boat and I was still out in the ocean floating on my back waiting for some strange fisherman to pick me up. Puking in front of strangers would've been less mortifying.

Wordlessly he handed me my toothbrush, wordlessly (obviously, it'd be hard to talk with a toothbrush in your mouth) I brushed, spit, and rinsed. Davis was there with a towel and a grin.

"Thanks," I mumbled.

"Bed."

Suddenly my nerves kicked in. This would be the first night I willfully got into bed with Davis. It was the first night I wasn't fully dressed. Not that I wasn't dressed at all, I was. I had on a silky PJ set that totally worked for a stay at the Four Seasons but seemed ridiculously extravagant for a beach cabana. I had never worn silk or anything similar. I was simple, my preferred nightwear was cotton or anything comfy. Not that the silk sleep set wasn't comfortable and soft but it was way too fancy for me. For some reason waking up in the morning wearing yesterday's clothes seemed like we were just friends who'd slept next to each other because we'd fallen asleep watching TV.

Getting into bed with a man was intimate.

Deliberate.

Deeply personal.

"In, baby," he said when he had the covers pulled back.

I put my knee onto the mattress but halted when Davis grabbed my wrist.

"You sure you're not going to be sick again?"

Great, now he was worried about me throwing up in bed.

Someone shoot me now.

"If you'd rather I sleep on the couch I can."

"I'd rather you climb into bed without looking like you're getting ready to be tortured."

Tortured would be the perfect description for what was going to happen in that bed.

"I'm not going to get sick."

Davis let go of my wrist. I finished getting into bed, then scooted as far as I could to the other edge, which wasn't far in a small double bed.

Damn.

Why was this so awkward?

"Jane—"

"I'm fine. This is just weird."

"Weird?"

"Us getting into bed together."

He stared down at me like I was the one who was weird, not the situation.

"We've slept together for the past two nights."

The reminder wasn't necessary.

"I know but this is different. We're getting into bed together, not just sleeping." When he didn't say anything I blathered on. "It's just…it feels…" I petered out because I didn't know how to explain it. "I've only slept beside three men in my entire life and one was my brother so he doesn't count. And I've only gotten into bed with two men and that includes you. That is, when you um…get into bed with me."

Davis did a slow blink and I seriously regretted admitting that.

"Come again?"

I didn't repeat myself mostly because I knew he heard and I was embarrassed as it was.

"You've only slept beside two men?"

Lord, why was my face so hot?

"Yes."

"And one of them is me?"

My cheeks now felt like they were on fire.

"Yes."

"Fuck," he snarled and turned to stomp to the bathroom.

What just happened?

I didn't have to wait long for Davis to come out of the

bathroom, tear off his shirt, and toss it on his backpack. Still angry, he told me, "Sometimes you shock me in ways that rip my heart apart."

That only confused me more.

"What?"

"Jane, you are just shy of forty and you've only slept next to two men."

Okay.

I was still confused.

"Baby." That came out frustrated and pained. "You gotta know we looked into you. I know you've never been married. We didn't find any long-term boyfriends so unless you hid him really well I know you haven't had one man in your bed for say, five, six, or ten years. Please tell me that you got a hang-up with sticking around after the deed is done and roll out and go home or kick him out."

Davis was still standing by the bed, which meant I had an unobstructed view of his beautiful chest. I was fully blaming my lack of concentration on that.

"The deed?"

"Fucking," he growled. "Please, God, tell me you kick him out of your house or you bounce when you're done."

"I don't kick men out of my bed, if that's what you mean."

"That's exactly what I mean."

Hold on a minute.

I sat up, focused on his squinty eyes, and gathered my thoughts.

"What kind of woman do you think I am, Davis?"

"I think you're a gorgeous, smart, sexy woman who I hope gets herself some and gets it regular. But if you're telling me you've slept next to two men and you don't kick 'em out when you're done, and I see the affront written all over you so I know you're rolling out of theirs, it's clear you're not. And since I'm one of the two men, and I haven't taken us there…*yet*, are you telling me you've only fucked one man?"

I was stuck on the, *I haven't taken us there…yet* part so I couldn't process what I'd confessed. No, that wasn't right, I could process it; I just wanted to ignore it until the end of time.

"Jane."

Damn it all to hell.

"Yes, Davis, that's what I'm saying."

"One? Just one?"

God, this was more mortifying than puking in front of him.

"Yes. One. Just one."

"Fuck," he rasped and tore his hands through his hair. "How the hell is that possible? You're fucking amazing."

That was a nice thing to say but…

"I hate to remind you of this but it was only a few days ago you didn't think I was amazing. You thought I was like Trevor and you're not the only one who's thought that."

A scary sinister look came over him.

"I didn't—"

"You did, Davis. You didn't like me and the only reason for you not to like me was because of who my brother is and I told you growing up everyone thought the same thing. By the time I got to high school it was assumed I was easy because I was the daughter of a biker. I was smart enough not to go there with anyone in high school. I had a bad reputation and I was a virgin. I couldn't imagine how bad it would've been if I'd fucked one of them. So I didn't. I stayed a virgin until my junior year of college. That relationship lasted a year and yes I slept next to him. After that I was back in CDA. No one paid me any mind being back there. I wasn't getting looks or comments so I kept to myself hoping that would last and it did."

Davis's gaze went to the floor and it remained there for so long I figured our conversation was over.

Without looking up he asked, "You haven't had sex in almost twenty years?"

I wasn't imagining the disbelief in his tone. It was there, clear as day and it pissed me off.

"You think I'm lying?"

Davis's head snapped up, his gaze found mine, and I felt the anger rolling off of him in hot waves.

"No, Jane, I don't think you're lying, I'm trying to gauge if I'm pissed off that you've been missing out on life, not having anyone in your bed, at your back, no one to make you feel good or if I'm one of the selfish fucks who's happy he scored himself a virgin."

"I'm not a virgin."

"Baby, you haven't had a man in twenty goddamn years, you might not technically be one but you damn well are."

I came up on my knees, felt my temper flare and my eyes get squinty.

"I'm not a virgin," I spat.

I saw it the moment the decision was made.

I just didn't understand what that decision was until Davis pounced.

"You damn well are," he ground out. "But you sure as fuck aren't going to be in a minute."

CHAPTER FIFTEEN

My mouth hit hers with bruising force. It was tongues and teeth—a clashing—feral, untamed, wild kiss. A kiss meant to claim ownership and I was damn well going to own every inch of her body.

A virgin.

Not technically but still…

Almost two decades without a man was pretty fucking close.

I still wasn't sure if I was seriously unhappy she'd gone so long without or if I was thrilled. However, I was sure I didn't give a fuck what it said about me that the thought I'd be the one to end her lonely dry spell made me want to thump my chest and howl at the moon like a caveman. This after I made good on my promise—I would ruin her. I'd make damn sure no one could ever make her feel as good as I could. I'd erase the memory of her college boyfriend. And I'd make damn sure the next time she was alone and getting herself off it would be my dick she was thinking about, my fingers, my tongue wrecking her.

But first I needed to slow this down.

I ended the kiss with a glide of my tongue.

She ended on a whimper.

Fucking perfect.

I opened my eyes in time to watch hers flutter open.

"You ready for more?" I asked while my hand skimmed up her waist, taking the silky material with it.

Jane's eyes went hooded, blatant desire danced in her stare. The nod was further indication she was with me, but I needed more.

"Say it."

"I want more," she whispered.

I rolled to my side, taking her with me, one arm going under her and the other over. Once I had her fitted tight to my chest my hand went back to gathering the silk and my lips went to her neck.

"You're in charge." I pressed a kiss under her ear as I pulled the flimsy material up, exposing her breasts. "You say when and how much."

Another nod accompanied by her wiggling her ass against my crotch.

"Say it."

"Say what?"

"What you want."

Jane arched her back in a nonverbal plea and normally that'd be enough for me but with her it wasn't. I wanted to hear the need in her voice.

"Use your words, baby."

"I…I can't."

"You can," I urged. "Tell me what you want me to do to your pretty tits."

"I don't know how."

She did, I'd seen the fire dancing in her eyes after our first kiss. She'd looked like she'd been ready to jump on my dick and I had very little doubt that if we'd been in private she would've done just that.

I just had to coax it out of her.

My hand trailed down over the swell of ample cleavage, stopping to thrum her stiff nipple, before I rolled it between my fingers and asked, "Tell me, Jane, do you want me to play here?"

"Yes."

"Yeah? Like this?" I rolled her nipple again, released it, then moved lower and grabbed a handful of her breast, massaging the soft flesh and went on. "Or this?"

"Both."

I smiled into the crook of her neck, licking and nibbling while I alternated between toying with her nipples and playing with her tits until she was squirming impatiently.

"You say when," I reminded her, "and how much."

"More."

"More of what? Of this?" I gave her breast a squeeze, then went to her nipple and pinched. "Or this?"

"Both. Harder. More."

I went back to playing, giving her more of what she asked for, this time not being as gentle as I'd been. Pinching and elongating her nipple until she whimpered. Digging my fingers in and squeezing her breast until she arched into my palm and moaned.

"More."

"Use your words, baby."

"More, Davis, I need more."

Then she'd get more.

"Are you wet for me?"

"Yes."

"How wet?"

Jane shoved her ass back against my erection.

"As sweet as your invitation is, I want to hear you ask."

"Touch me."

Christ.

Beautiful.

Soft, warm skin slid under my palm as my hand made its way down her stomach. I dipped under the band of her shorts, cupped her pussy over her panties, and kissed her neck.

"Hitch your leg over my hip." I waited until Jane opened herself to me then decided to have pity. "I'm gonna fuck you with my fingers until you come. While I'm doing that I want your arms up so I can play with your pussy and your tits."

I rolled back just enough to give her the space she needed to comply. When she did I traced the seam of her pussy over her panties. I continued to tease until Jane started to make frustrated sounds. I filed those away for later knowing damn good and well I could jerk off to the memory of her making those noises and get there in seconds.

"Davis," she snapped. "The finger-fucking."

Okay, I was wrong. I could jack off and shoot off remembering her angry demand for my fingers, and do that harder and faster than anything else in my vast arsenal of jerk-off material.

Without making her wait any longer I shoved my hand into her panties, skimmed the tips of my fingers over her clit on my way down, and didn't stop until I had two fingers deep in her pussy.

I stilled, closed my eyes, and breathed in a lungful of oxygen in an attempt not to lose control.

"Davis," she groaned.

I still didn't move.

"Give me a second."

Jane went stiff and I realized my mistake.

"Baby, your pussy is so fucking hot, so wet, all I can think about is how good it's gonna feel when I sink inside you. I want this to be good for you so I need a second to find my control before I forget the finger-fucking, roll you over, and you get acquainted with my dick in a way that's gonna have you screaming until you're hoarse."

Jane squirmed and rocked her hips.

"I want that," she breathed.

"Trust me when I tell you, you're not ready for that."

With that, I curled my fingers and commenced giving her something she could handle knowing that I still didn't have a lock on my control. But the need to hear her moaning in pleasure took precedence. Jane didn't disappoint; within minutes she was bucking against my hand, grinding her clit into my palm. Though she wasn't moaning, she was begging.

"Please, honey."

"Please what?"

"Harder."

I blocked out how much my dick liked that idea, plunged my fingers deeper and harder, secured my arm around her ribs, and settled in for the show, watching her tits bounce in time with my thrusts.

"I'm gonna…"

Jane trailed off and moaned her orgasm.

I shoved my face in her neck and stroked her through it until the tightness left and she sagged in my arms.

I could say that lying there with Jane in my arms, my dick hard and throbbing, my fingers up her cunt, her tits resting on my forearm, and her breaths still coming fast and choppy I'd never been more sated.

Satisfied in a way I'd never been in my life.

"Davis?"

"Yeah, baby?"

"I'm ready for more."

She might've been but I wasn't sure I could go gentle.

"I could eat," I murmured against the side of her neck.

"Huh?"

"Your pussy, baby," I told her and unlocked my hold around her before I gave her her options. "On your back or do you want to ride my face?"

Jane shook her head but remained quiet.

It took several long moments but she shocked the hell out of me and announced, "I want to ride your dick."

My dick was wholeheartedly on board with that plan.

Fortunately the days when my dick ruled my body were long past.

"I want to taste you first," I denied, hoping when I was done giving her another orgasm she'd be drained and ready for sleep.

There was more silence. For Jane's sudden burst of confidence, I should've braced when her hand went to my arm, then slid down until she curled her fingers around my wrist and tugged my hand out of her panties. She lifted my hand and brought it up toward my face.

"Open your mouth," she demanded.

Obediently I did her bidding, then just as obediently I sucked my fingers into my mouth, tasting her climax.

"Now you've tasted me."

Shit, *fuck*.

Need flooded my bloodstream. My body heated, my dick throbbed, my control unraveled.

In an attempt to regain rational thought, I wrapped my hand around her wrist and pulled my now-clean fingers out of my mouth.

"Jane—"

"I want your dick."

Welp, that fucking did it.

Apparently, Jane had better control over my body than I did.

I rolled to my back taking her with me, cupped her face, and held her where I wanted her.

"You control this, but warning, I'm nearing my breaking point. I need to know you're ready for this. If you're not, crawl up and let me eat you."

Jane's lips tipped up, not in a sweet smile, but in a grin that stated clearly she knew what she was doing to me.

"Your need for consent is—"

"Straight up, I need to know where you're at and you're with me every step. But your body, you moaning and begging for my dick tells me everything I need to know. I trust you to speak up if we go somewhere you don't want to go. I'm not gonna ask every two seconds if you're good."

"Earlier you wanted me to say it."

Now it was my turn to smile.

"Yeah, baby, because hearing you tell me you want to ride my dick is hot as fuck. Here's another warning for you, I'm gonna want to hear that again. I'm gonna make you use filthy words to ask for all sorts of things and I'm going to do that because it turns me on. I get off on it. It makes me want to fuck you until you can't breathe. And that brings us back to my first warning—I want to fuck you breathless. I'm not sure I can be gentle with you and I don't want to hurt you."

"Hurt me?"

"Jane, you haven't—"

"You won't hurt me."

She had no idea.

I let go of her face and placed my hands on the bed.

"Sit up."

A confused look passed over her features but she did as I asked and settled back on my lap. Just that small amount of friction had me grinding my teeth.

"Hands on my chest."

She did that, too.

"What do you feel?"

Jane tipped her chin and tilted her head.

"Tell me, Jane, what do you feel?"

"You're…you're shaking," she stammered.

"Yeah, do you get it now?"

"I think so."

No, she didn't get it.

"I'm lying under you literally shaking with the need to get inside of you. Vibrating with it. I can't promise you I'll go gentle. I can't promise because I've never felt this and it's scaring the shit out of me thinking I'll hurt you."

Jane's eyes went half-mast, her mouth went soft, and her hand flexed on my chest.

"You won't hurt me," she said and leaned forward to brush her lips over mine. "And since you want the filthy words, how about this?" She paused and sucked in a breath. I braced and it was a damn good thing I did. "I want to ride you until I come then I want you to ride me until you do."

Jesus, fuck.

The growl that crawled up my chest came out as vicious as it felt.

"Roll off me, clothes off. *Now.*"

I saw her smile that smile that said she knew she owned my body—my dick in particular.

Jane rolled off, tore her shirt off, shimmied out of her shorts and panties, then rolled back to yank my shorts down my legs. The woman wasn't playing, though her gaze did linger on my dick once she'd freed it before she threw her leg over my waist and balanced on her knees over me.

I kept my hands on the bed, fisted the sheets, and ordered, "Ride me."

She didn't move but her eyes roamed my face, my neck, and my chest before they came back and met mine.

"You're beautiful," she whispered.

I felt my muscles constrict. But more than that I felt my heart rate tick up.

Christ.

"When I first saw you in front of the bakery," she kept going as she reached down, wrapped her soft hand around my very hard dick, then finished with, "I thought you were the most beautiful man I'd ever seen."

Good Christ.

I could do nothing but glory in the feel of her tight, wet pussy as she sank down on my cock. I had no choice seeing as if I moved a single muscle I was going to flip her and take what I wanted.

"Jesus," I grunted.

Staring down at me with a desire-filled gaze she slid up then dropped back down. Over and over she rode me slowly. It was pure fucking torture. Every glide drove me closer to losing it.

"Faster, baby," I gritted out.

She went faster.

My eyes dropped to her big, heavy tits tipped with pink, pebbled nipples and watched them bounce.

"Faster," I begged and let go of the sheets to grip her hips. "Lean back, brace your hands on my thighs, and fuck me hard, Jane. You've got two more minutes and playtime's over."

"I don't need two minutes," she groaned.

As it turned out she didn't even need a full minute before she slammed down, rocked her hips, and climaxed on a shout.

Fucking hell.

With her pussy convulsing, threatening to undo me, I flipped her and took over.

"You on the pill?"

"No."

Fuck.

I pulled out, took my dick in hand, and stroked. On the third pump with my eyes locked with Jane's I went off, marking her stomach with my come.

Then I gave her what I should've given her when she told me she thought I was beautiful.

"You have the most beautiful eyes I've ever seen. When you're pissed they spark with fire. When you're turned on they go hazy and get deep green. When you come you lose focus and your eyelids flutter—it's the sexiest thing I've ever seen. You're beautiful with short blonde hair and you're stunning with long brown. Top to toe, baby, you're just plain gorgeous."

My gaze dropped to her stomach, the evidence of my orgasm painting her soft, tanned skin and I kept going.

"You've got the sweetest pussy I've ever had. You feel phenomenal, the sounds you make drive me crazy and when you fuck me slow and gentle it's goddamn torture. But it's good to know I got it in me to keep a lock on my control because we're gonna test that again."

"Torture?" she whispered.

I lifted my gaze to meet hers.

"Pure. Fucking. Torture. Every glide of your pussy felt so damn good I thought I was going to lose my mind. Watching my dick sink in and come out coated with your excitement drove me closer to the edge. You going slow, drawing that out, the best kind of torture."

"As compliments go that was crass but thanks."

"Yeah, baby, it was crass but it was real. This is me. I know what I like, I have no problem getting it and so I have no problem saying it straight. What I need you to know is with me, in our bed, you are safe to be you. You can do and say whatever feels good to you. Anything goes."

Those pretty eyes went hazy and the green deepened.

I knew what that meant.

"How ya feeling?" I asked.

"Ruined."

I closed my eyes and let that wash over me.

When I opened them, I lowered my mouth to hers.

"That makes two of us."

I heard her gasp right before I took her mouth.

After that, I fucked her breathless.

Just to make sure she remembered in a way she could never forget who she belonged to.

Corinne Lawrence might've been the daughter of Satan but Jane Wright was the reigning Queen.

And she'd be that long after the devil was put down.

CHAPTER SIXTEEN

I watched Davis come in from the porch, phone still to his ear. I held up the coffee pot in a silent question.

He brought his mug to the counter and set it down next to mine. I warmed his up and heard, "The later flight would be better." He paused to kiss my temple before going back to his conversation. "Who's taking us to the airport?"

Airport.

Oh, shit, we're going home.

I glanced down at my mug and waited for the fear to infuse me but none came.

Yesterday Wilson had reported that my father had been "defused"—Wilson's word, not mine. I'd never known my father to be defused or denied anything but I was trusting that Wilson knew what he was talking about. But I knew it wasn't my trust in Wilson that kept my fears at bay, it was Davis. He wouldn't agree to go back to Idaho if he didn't know I'd be safe.

"He has everything for Jane?"

Right. I'd need a driver's license to fly, something I didn't need for our marriage license because that had been arranged by Wilson.

"We'll be ready," he finished. "Jane?"

"Yeah?" I lifted my head and found he was close.

"You okay?"

"Yeah."

"You know I'd never take you back if it wasn't safe."

See?

There it was.

I knew Davis.

"I know."

"Then why do you look…" he zeroed in on my eyes and continued, "sad?"

Sad was a good word for what I was.

I was also disappointed our time had come to an end.

"It's beautiful here." I shrugged.

I knew Davis wasn't buying it when he stepped closer, hooked me around the waist, and pulled me to his side.

His head tipped down, mine tipped up, and he muttered, "Baby?"

God, why did he have to be so damn hot when he was being sweet?

"Okay, fine, I'm sad. Kind of. I'm just disappointed we're going home and our time together is over."

"Over?" he asked, his arm around me getting super tight.

"Well, yeah. We're going back to Idaho."

"What does that have to do with our time being over?"

I wasn't sure how to answer that. We hadn't exactly talked about what was happening when we got home. So, I asked him.

"What's happening?"

"What's happening?" he mumbled under his breath. "What's happening is we're going home—*together*."

It was my turn to mumble under my breath though mine

was more of a breathy sigh because *together* meant maybe our time wasn't over.

"What?"

"Jane, we're married."

Fake married.

My heart clenched and I dipped my chin to study the floor. Davis didn't allow this for long. Ever so gently he grabbed my chin and forced me to refocus on him.

"Jane?"

"Huh?"

My heart got tighter in my chest when Davis's expression went funny. Not guarded, not irritated. It was full-on concern but something else, too, and I couldn't put my finger on it.

"You good?"

"Why wouldn't I be?"

"With last night, baby, you good with how that went down?"

Was I good with being ruined for all other men for all of eternity?

Yes.

Was I good with Davis making good on his promise to fuck me breathless?

Hell to the yes.

Was I good with round three when Davis kissed and/or licked every inch of my body to the point I was breathless again but felt cherished and adored?

That was a big hell yes.

Was I good with how it started?

I hadn't been but I couldn't deny the results of my admission that I'd only had sex with one man didn't end with a spectacular outcome. That being me ending a self-imposed dry spell to end all dry spells with too many orgasms to count and waking up the next morning next to the beautiful man who'd given them to me, feeling used in all the best ways.

"Yeah," I answered, suddenly feeling shy.

Davis being Davis was not shy when he pushed. "Baby, I was rough with you last night."

"Yes, I was there, I remember." I smiled.

"I'm being serious, Jane."

He looked like he was very serious.

He'd been honest with me and he'd proven I could be honest with him but still it was hard.

Old habits and all that jazz…

I sucked in a breath.

"Last night was great—all of it. I'm just worried—"

Davis tightened his arm around me and interrupted with, "Last night was *great*?"

"Yeah." I drew out the word, confused.

Did *he* not think it was great?

"Uh, no," he clipped. "Last night wasn't *great*; it was fucking phenomenal. Told you that last night but now I'm seeing you didn't get me so let me explain again."

Davis dipped down just enough so we were eye to eye and there was no avoiding his stare. Which meant what came next was done in a way I couldn't ever forget.

"I like you. I like the way we connected. I think you got that part, but if you didn't I'll recap and remind you. I enjoyed every second, every moan, the way you clawed at my back, the way you felt, tasted, gave, and took. Start to finish, unbelievably phenomenal. I seriously like your mouth and how you kiss. I'm looking forward to getting your mouth around my dick and watching you suck me off. But beyond all of that, I told you I wanted real."

Davis gave me another squeeze and went on. "I meant that in bed and out of it. I don't want you holding back or hiding. If you have something to say—say it. If you're not sure about something—ask."

"We're fake married," I blurted out.

Davis did a slow blink.

"So I wasn't sure what was happening when we got home. Like, do we just go back to our separate lives? Do we exchange phone numbers and keep in touch?"

A sexy smile pulled at his lips.

"Yeah, baby, we're gonna keep in touch."

Why did that thrill and sadden me at the same time?

Thankfully Davis didn't make me ask for the ins and outs of the ways we were going to keep in touch.

"Mia and Cole already moved your stuff into my place. Not your furniture but your clothes and shit."

"My clothes and shit?"

"Don't know what shit Mia packed, but Cole told me the whole time she was in your bathroom she was waxing poetic about your perfume collection and Mia was snapping pictures of the bottles."

I had a serious addiction to perfume.

"I like the pretty bottles," I sheepishly told him.

"Not sure why you look like you're embarrassed. There's nothing wrong with liking pretty things even if it's bottles of perfume."

He wasn't wrong about that so I went back to the moving in part.

"I'm moving in with you?"

"Fake married or not, you're my wife. We're living this real."

I wasn't sure my heart could take living it real with Davis. I was already too invested.

"Right," I murmured.

"Jane," he impatiently snapped. "If you have something to say, *say it*."

God, he was annoying.

"Fine," I returned, matching his tone. "I'll *say it*. I'm scared."

"Your father—"

"I'm not scared of *him*. Well, that's a lie, he scares me because he's an asshole and unpredictable and I know he's not done fucking with me or my brother but if you tell me I'm safe to go home I believe you."

"Then what are you scared of?"

"You!"

Davis flinched.

"Me? So I did hurt—"

"No, you big dummy, I'm scared I'm going to fall in love with you. I'm scared that I'm already falling, and going home and playing house with you is going to make me fall more. I'm scared that living it real will make me forget it's fake. I'm scared when this is over I won't want to stop being your wife."

My admission was met with silence.

Silence in words but not in action.

As I was finding with Davis, he was good at communicating his feelings and not just verbally. Truth be told, I liked when he said it straight but when he showed me I liked it a whole lot more. So when his mouth came down and his tongue tangled with mine I melted into his kiss.

When he broke away he stayed close, and with a whispered growl that sent shivers up my spine he asked, "Did that feel fake?"

"No," I whispered back.

"We're living this real, and while we are I'll have a mind to where you are. But just so you know, I'm right there with you."

Before I could stop myself I squeaked, "You are?"

"Do we need to have another conversation about last night?"

Perhaps my earlier thoughts were in haste; sometimes Davis's straight talk freaked me out.

"No."

"I think we do."

Oh, boy.

"We don't—"

"You're gorgeous," he stated, and that felt nice. But I sensed he wasn't paying me a compliment. "You're loyal, even if those loyalties are totally fucked, you still can't help yourself. The love you give the same."

I didn't know where this was going but I didn't like it. I opened my mouth to tell him just that when he lifted his hand and pressed his thumb against my lips. I really didn't like that and felt my eyes narrow.

"I like that. I don't like the man who's on the receiving end, but I like that you have that in you and I understand it even if I disagree."

He was still pressing on my lips so my, "how great for you" came out distorted.

"I'm saying that to mean a woman like you, who's held herself distant for decades doesn't give herself to a man unless she's falling. So I already knew before you told me. But it's good to have you confirm. It's also good I get to tell you I'm feeling the same. I don't bullshit. I don't lie. I don't play games. I wouldn't have taken us where we went last night if I wasn't all in. If I didn't want to explore where this is going, and I didn't want *real*. You with me on this now?"

His thumb brushed over my bottom lip, then over my cheek, and he waited for me to answer.

"Yes."

"You sure?"

"Yeah."

"Good. Now I'm gonna fuck you again before we have to pack."

I felt another shiver glide up my spine.

Davis wasted no time getting down to business. I was up in his arms for the ten steps it took him to get to the bed then the skirt of my dress was bunched at my waist and Davis was lowering himself to his knees next to the side of the bed while dragging my panties off.

"Whoever had the foresight to buy you nothing but dresses is getting a case of their favorite hooch."

I smiled at the ceiling.

Davis opened my legs, traced the seam of my sex with his thumbs.

I lifted my head off the bed and looked down to find him looking at me, his face openly hungry.

Davis Wright on his knees for *me*.

The sight was so hot I trembled.

I didn't get a chance to process why I liked that so much before his mouth closed over my pussy and he went at me. There were no soft flicks or lazy build up. Davis's fingertips dug into my thighs and he tongue-fucked me deep.

I cried out, my hands went to his head, and I rocked into his mouth. I was close and getting closer when he pulled away.

My protest died when he surged to his feet, rolled me to my belly, yanked me to the edge of the mattress, got me on my knees, and in one thrust drove his big, thick dick deep.

My head flew up, my back bowed, and I panted through his driving thrusts. One of his hands slid around, down, and hit his target with shocking accuracy.

He toyed with my clit.

I writhed.

I chanted his name.

I attempted to meet his thrusts but it was too much.

All of it.

This wasn't fucking.

This was a claiming.

He wanted real and this was his way of communicating that.

It was as beautiful as it was brutal.

"Davis," I breathed as my climax started to sear through me.

He pounded deeper, faster, his breaths now labored as he fucked me through my orgasm.

"Honey," I mewled.

"Thank fuck," he grunted.

Davis pulled out and suddenly my pussy was clutching at nothing. His finger left my clit, went to the back of my neck, slid down to my shoulder blades, and he put pressure there. I caught his meaning, lowered my upper torso to the bed, leaving my ass up and on display. I turned my head enough to watch him finish himself off. I groaned when the first jet of warm come hit my ass.

"Fuck," he groaned and closed his eyes.

My orgasm was great, his looked better.

His hand slowed and his eyes opened. When they did they immediately found mine.

"Need to get on the pill, baby."

He was correct. I did.

Though I liked him marking me so maybe I didn't.

I liked it more when he rubbed the head of his dick over the mess he'd made on my ass.

"Love seeing me on you."

It was good we agreed on that.

"Yeah," I whispered and watched.

"We straight about earlier?"

Davis wanted real.

He'd told me, shown me, and now he wanted confirmation I was with him.

I wanted to ask him if he was real or if he was a figment of my imagination. No man was as perfect as him. At least not the men I'd grown up around or any of the men I'd met.

"We're straight about earlier."

"Good. Now we gotta clean up and get packed."

I didn't want to get packed. I wanted a nap and maybe round two.

"Okay."

I started to move but stopped when Davis bent over me, pinning me to the bed. His mouth went to my cheek, his lips brushed a sweet kiss there, then they moved to my ear.

"Stick with me, Jane, and I promise, I fucking vow I'll keep you safe. Not just from your father and brother. You'll be safe to be you and while you're doing that your heart's safe with me, too."

I felt tears prick the backs of my eyes.

I hoped with everything inside of me that Davis Wright kept that promise. Because in that moment I fell headfirst in love with him.

"I'll stick with you," I promised.

Davis went solid, but I felt him smile.

His smile felt great.

"Seal the deal."

I had no idea what he meant until his mouth moved to mine and the kiss he gave me rivaled all the ones that had come before.

Though, it slipped into the first place slot of being the best kiss of my life because Davis was again showing me in the best of ways I could trust him.

CHAPTER SEVENTEEN

Three stops and sixteen hours later we were in gray and gloomy Spokane waiting for Wilson to pick us up from the airport.

"I already miss the sun," Jane mumbled.

I spotted Wilson's SUV thinking I would have to take her back to a beach soon.

"I missed out on seeing you in a bikini."

Jane jolted next to me and her body started shaking with soft laughter.

"Yeah, well, I missed out on seeing you in trunks. Though, maybe it's a good thing you didn't get a chance to show off your superior good looks while shirtless on the beach."

"Superior good looks?"

Without looking at me she shook her head and said, "Please, like you don't know you're hot and have a great body."

"Didn't say that, just pleased you think so. This is us." I unwrapped my arm from around her shoulders but found her hand to guide her to where Wilson had pulled over.

When I realized I was dragging her I stopped and looked over at her.

"What's wrong?"

"Nothing."

"Jane," I warned.

"You know, sometimes you're annoying," she snapped. "I'm fine."

"Baby, I'm dragging you to the car. That's not fine."

"I'm just nervous. Sheesh, do you have to know my every thought?"

Without hesitation and uncaring we had an audience, I cupped her face and brought it close to mine.

"When you're nervous, scared, or unsure, yes, I need to know your every thought. When you're happy, excited, feeling good, yes, I want to know that, too. The first so I can find a way to help you. The second so I can figure out how to keep doing whatever it is that's making you feel those things so I can continue to do them."

Jane's features softened, those pretty green eyes gazing into mine like I'd handed her something special. I didn't get to fully appreciate how good that felt before I heard a throat clear. My eyes sliced to the side and I saw Wilson's lips twitch.

"Jane's nervous so don't be a dick."

I felt rather than heard Jane's swift inhale but I very much heard her hiss, "I can't believe you said that."

I glanced back at Jane and without a tinge of remorse declared, "Believe it."

"Davis!"

I ignored Jane and went back to Wilson.

"Ready?"

"You tell me," he returned.

"We're ready."

I followed Wilson to the curb, this time not bothering to question why Jane was still dragging her feet. I opened the door, stepped to the side, and tipped my head down.

"That wasn't cool," she chastised.

"Are you still nervous?"

"No."

I lifted my brow in a silent *you're welcome*.

Jane didn't feel very appreciative.

"But now I'm embarrassed."

"Why would you be embarrassed?"

Jane let out a sigh and glanced around. What she didn't do was answer.

"Jane?"

"This is hard for me. Everyone knows who my brother is."

Fuck.

"No one is going to judge you for his actions. Everyone knows you have nothing to do with his club."

She gave me a look that stated clearly she thought I was full of shit.

So I did the only thing I could do—I leaned forward, gave her a quick, hard, closed mouth kiss, and helped her into the back of the SUV.

When I had her settled, I stayed bent close.

"This is something you're gonna have to see for yourself to believe. But I promise you, everyone will be cool with you."

I closed the door and got in.

Wilson immediately launched in. "Brace, brother. River's taken a turn and has gone from crazy to certifiably insane."

I smiled. "Letty's getting close."

"Right, but River's acting like she's birthing the next messiah."

I couldn't say for sure since I'd never had a pregnant wife, therefore I didn't know how I would react, but I was thinking I'd probably be like River.

Crazy in the beginning and insane by the end.

"Letty's his whole world."

I didn't say anymore because that said it all.

"What else has been going on?"

Wilson spent the next forty-five minutes filling me in on other cases we'd been working on and closed since I'd been gone. Throughout this I periodically checked on Jane. The first few times she'd given me small smiles that came nowhere near real. The last time I'd checked, her head was resting back and her eyes were closed.

We were off the freeway headed up 41 North through Post Falls when I asked, "How do you know Kai?"

"I don't. He's a friend of a friend I worked with at Homeland. Got lucky with that."

Indeed we had.

Wilson lowered his voice and continued, "He called, told me what happened with his son. Wiped the bill for your stay and the car he was letting you use and said if we ever needed him again he was on standby." There was a pause. "He lost his wife a few years ago, that's why he moved from Maui to Lanai. I don't know him, but I don't need to, to know he's grateful."

"It was a right time, right place situation. The kid was fishing alone and got caught in his net when he got into the water to untangle it from some debris. And that was Jane, not me, who saw him."

"Then it's a damn good thing she was there."

There was nothing to say to that so I didn't reply. But I was thinking about life and how one decision can go on to impact someone else's life. If Jane hadn't insisted we leave the Four Seasons she wouldn't have been on the porch to see Noah. If we'd stayed inside instead of going out to that porch a boy could've died less than five hundred yards away while we enjoyed our coffee.

"The butterfly effect," I mumbled.

"Come again?"

"One seemingly meaningless decision had saved Noah."

That was life; simple occurrences that rippled until they touched someone else.

"Cole's rubbing off on you."

"Fuck off."

Wilson was still chuckling when he turned into my development. It was not my first choice of places to live. I much preferred to be out where Rhode and Brooklyn lived, surrounded by acres of nature. Or like Reese and his log cabin with fewer acres than Rhode, but still he had land. But when I was looking I couldn't find anything I'd liked so I settled on a house in a development with neighbors so close we could hold a conversation standing on our back patios and not have to raise our voices.

I was saving to build a house.

Which reminded me, I still had to give Wilson the rest of the fifty K I owed him.

I didn't get the chance to tell him I'd transfer the money before I saw a line of familiar cars.

"Jesus," I grumbled.

"You've been gone a long time," Wilson noted, "and you've come home with a wife. What did you expect?"

"What's wrong?" Jane's sleepy voice came from behind me.

"Nothing, baby, we have company but I'll get rid of them."

"Why would you get rid of your friends?"

Was she not there less than an hour ago when she told me she was nervous?

"We just spent half a day getting home. They can come visit after you've settled and you're comfortable."

There were a few beats of silence before she asked, "Will they be mean to me?"

"Fuck no."

"They're your friends. Why would you kick them out of your house?"

I glanced over my shoulder and held Jane's sleepy gaze.

"Because this is now your home and I want you comfortable. But so I won't be rude, they can stay for ten minutes, then I'm kicking them out so you can rest."

"Good luck with that," Wilson mumbled. "I think Rhode said something about smoking a brisket and Letty said she was craving baked beans so Mia jumped on that. Sadie was talking about you needing a proper wedding cake so there might be that, too."

I glanced at my friend.

He was grinning like an idiot.

"You think maybe you should've mentioned all of this to me back at the airport?"

"Nope. I thought it would be fun to see the look on your face when you saw the cars. And I wasn't wrong, it was amusing."

I refrained from calling him a dick but just barely and only because Jane was now fully awake and I didn't want her thinking something was wrong.

As soon as Wilson pulled into my driveway the vultures descended to the front lawn.

"Um." I heard Jane mutter. "That's a lot of friends."

Brooklyn, Remy, Mia, Cole, Asher, Sloane, and River had filed out.

"That's not all of them. We're missing Rhode and Letty and depending on who they invited, Letty's parents Michael and Tallulah and Mrs. Simpson could also be here."

"Affirmative. Michael, Tally, and Mrs. S were all invited."

"Christ," I bit out.

"JESUS," I muttered under my breath when I saw all the decorations.

Purple, silver, and white shiny streamers hung vertically. Blocking the back window. In front of it, a wooden sign that said *Mr. & Mrs.* was draped across the streamers. My dining room table had a purple tablecloth with vases of cream peonies and violet hydrangeas. There were balloons dotting the ceiling. The house smelled like candles were burning mixed with freshly baked cookies.

"Surprise," Tally called as she came into the living room.

"Welcome home," Letty said, trailing behind her mother.

"Jesus," I repeated, this time getting a good look at a very, very pregnant Letty. "How many kids do you have in there?"

Letty flipped me off before she snapped, "Have you met my husband?"

My eyes sliced to the six-foot-three powerhouse that was River Kent then back to Letty.

"Fair enough," I conceded.

"Now that you've pointed out I'm as big as a house will you please introduce me to your wife?"

Jane went stiff and I curled my arm tighter around her waist.

"Letty, this is Jane. Jane, Letty. She's married to River, the big guy over there." River gave a jerk of his chin then I went on. "Everyone else, this is Jane and you're on your own explaining who belongs to who or this will take a year."

"Oh, for goodness sakes, boy, where are your manners?" Mrs. Simpson said from the couch. "Come here, child, and I'll introduce you around."

Jane made no attempt to leave my side. As a matter of fact she shoved closer as Reese's wife Sadie made her way to us.

"Hey, Jane," Sadie softly said. "I don't know if you remember me. We went to Fernan together. Sadie Pierce. Well, it's Sadie Turmel now but it was Pierce back then."

"You remember me?"

Suddenly it hit me, something Jane had said the day I'd met her.

They paint me with the same brush, thinking they know me, then do exactly what you did, and judge me.

Surely sweet Sadie was not one of her classmates who judged her.

I pulled Jane tighter against my side.

"Um…" Sadie stopped and clasped her hands in front of her, seemingly unsure of herself and what to say.

What the fuck?

I'd never seen Sadie at a loss for words or unsure about anything.

"It's okay," Jane rushed to fill the silence.

"What's okay?" I asked.

Jane's head turned and her eyes tipped up to meet mine.

"That she remembers me. I mean, I remember her, too. We were only a few grades apart."

"So we can get this out of the way," Sadie said and both Jane and I looked back at her. "I remembered who you were when you first came into my bakery but you didn't seem to remember me so I didn't bring it up. I wouldn't have said anything now except I think it's uncool to start a friendship on a lie. And since we're going to be friends I wanted you to know I remember you from elementary school."

There was the sweet Sadie I knew. I loosened my arm and Jane relaxed.

"I remember you," Jane admitted. "I actually didn't think you recognized me when I went into your bakery and I was grateful because I didn't want you to kick me out since your cinnamon rolls are the best in Coeur d'Alene."

"Kick you out? Why in the world would I kick you out?"

"Because my brother's—"

"So the hell what? My brother's a member of the Horsemen. You're not Zeus and I'm not Grinder."

Jane turned to stone.

"Are you going to let your wife meet the rest of us or are you going to hog her?" Letty impatiently snapped.

I dropped my arm, found Jane's hand, and tugged. I didn't stop tugging until we were back out on my front porch.

"Your call," I started. "I can go back in there and tell everyone we're tired and we can do this tomorrow, or you can meet my team and their women. No pressure and it's up to you. The only thing I'll say is, Sadie said it true—you are not Zeus and she is not Grinder. No one in my house will disrespect or—"

I stopped talking when Jane's hand came up and her knuckles brushed my jaw.

"Thank you."

What the hell was she thanking me for? I'd unwittingly walked her into an ambush.

"I was nervous, now I'm not."

"You're not?" I stupidly asked.

"Nope. How can I be nervous when I know I have you to—"

I didn't let her finish.

I bent down and kissed my wife.

Unfortunately this was interrupted by a very rambunctious, very loud six-year-old.

"They're kissing!" Remy shouted.

"Get away from the window, Remington!" I heard Rhode yell.

"But I'm hungry."

Slowly I broke the kiss and rested my forehead on Jane's.

"Ready to go in?"

"Yeah."

"They're done!" Remy announced.

"Cockblocker," I muttered.

Jane tried, she really did, and I knew it when she started to sputter. I also knew she'd lost the battle when she busted out laughing.

Beautiful.

Now she was ready to go back inside.

"Welcome home, baby."

CHAPTER EIGHTEEN

"You gonna come for me, baby?" Davis asked.

This was done with a rough, scratchy voice that was partly due to us having just woken up before I wiggled back into his morning hard-on. Davis happily accepted my invitation and was on his side behind me, holding my leg over his hip, taking me nice and slow.

"Yes," I breathed.

"Need my finger at your clit?"

I absolutely did not need his finger at my clit. He was making magic playing with my nipple.

I shook my head the best I could with his face in my neck and arched into my climax. Davis continued to give me both his dick and nipple action, taking me through a slow, sweet release that curled my toes.

When it moved through me, he pulled out and left his mark on my ass.

"We really need to get you on the pill," he reiterated yesterday's statement. "Or I need to glove up."

"No. I like the feel of you. Just you, nothing between us. I'll get on the pill."

Davis gently rolled me to my back. He traced his finger from my throat, down between my breasts, and stopped to circle my belly button. He looked like he had something on his mind beyond protection.

"You okay?"

"Perfect."

"Then why the forlorn look?"

Davis blinked then smiled.

"Forlorn?"

"Don't pretend you don't know what that means and don't try to change the subject."

"I like waking up next to you."

His words were accompanied by his hand gliding back up. This time his route took his palm over my ribs, the side of my breast, and finally he brushed my hair away from my face.

Oh, yeah, Davis was really good with the tell and show.

I liked that so much I nuzzled his hand in my hair, which was now cupping the side of my head.

"So why do you look solemn?"

"How's a man supposed to look when he's got exactly what he wants in his bed, in his life, and he's worried she won't stay?"

Davis said that—straight out. No games. No hiding. He just put that right out there between us.

Was he for real?

How could he be real?

"You know you're perfect, right?" I whispered. "So perfect it's scary."

"How can perfect be scary?"

I paused just long enough to push aside the lessons of my youth and give Davis what he'd given me—total, unfiltered honesty.

"I told you I was falling. You promised you'd be gentle with me and I believe you. I believe that when you grow tired of me, you'll be kind about it. You won't hurt me when you let me go but in the back of my mind I can't help wondering if one day, when all this is over, if you'll realize I'm not good…"

I petered out when Davis's eyes narrowed dangerously and his brows pinched.

"Finish what you were going to say."

"Umm…"

"Smart," he muttered. "I like waking up to you," he repeated.

"I like waking up to you," I parroted.

An obnoxious chime rang out.

Davis made a sound that was a cross between an angry grunt and a growl.

"You've got to be shitting me," he verbally expressed his anger as he rolled and craned his neck to look at the nightstand.

I didn't know what time it was but the sun was blaring into his bedroom so it couldn't have been early.

The chime went off again and Davis rolled the rest of the way off the bed, tagged yesterday's jeans off the floor, and stepped into them while saying, "I'll get the door. Start coffee and come back and I'll join you in the shower."

Guess I was taking a shower.

"And we'll finish our conversation over breakfast."

I had a smart-ass quip prepared but didn't get to fire it off before he was out the bedroom door—or more accurately, *prowled* out the door.

I took my time getting out of bed, savoring the soreness between my legs. Davis had argued I'd reverted back to being a virgin since my self-imposed celibacy had lasted through my twenties and well into my thirties. Technically he was wrong, however I couldn't disagree with his sentiment. After all the sex we'd had I couldn't deny I was a whole lot of out of practice and a little sore. Not that I was complaining. Hell, if my college boyfriend had been as good as Davis I wasn't sure I would've been satisfied with self-induced orgasms over the years—reputation be damned.

And, really, thinking about it, for a woman who said she didn't care what other people thought of her I sure had wasted a lot of time and energy caring what other people thought. I'd denied myself pleasure and connections because I'd been too afraid I'd be judged. I'd put myself through college, graduated, came home, worked, and that was it.

No life.

No friends.

Nothing.

I was a fraud and a liar and I wasn't sure what to make of that but it bore contemplation. Just not right now. I had plans this afternoon with Letty and Brooklyn and I was determined not to allow my past to get in the way of my future. I knew Davis played a large role in this new determination but I didn't care. He made me feel good. He looked at me like I was Jane.

Just Jane.

Me, or the me I wanted to be.

Deep down I knew I wasn't like my brother or father. I knew I was a good person but that didn't mean I hadn't allowed their dysfunction to pull me under.

I like you in my bed.

Davis thought he had what he wanted in his bed and in his life.

That had to mean something.

He was the best man I'd ever met.

If he thought I was worthy of being at his side, I was going to prove him right or I was going to lose him.

I was coasting on these thoughts when I got out of bed.

This was not a 'fake it until you make it' sort of thing. It was a 'the time is nigh to start living life' thing and since I wanted to do that with Davis the time wasn't only nigh—it was upon me.

I glanced around Davis's bedroom. Much like the rest of his house it was nicely decorated with a bent toward masculine which made sense. He was a bachelor, though the furniture was so nice I wondered if he'd picked it out or if one of the women had helped him…or maybe an ex.

Nope.

I wasn't going there.

My guess was Letty. She was ballsy and bossy with a huge side of hilarious. I could see her taking charge of furnishing Davis's home.

Low, rumbling voices caught my attention. I moved closer to the open door and listened. I couldn't make out what was being said but Davis sounded ticked and the other voice sounded like my brother.

Oh, shit.

Shit.

Shit.

Shit.

I grabbed Davis's shirt off the floor, yanked it on, found my panties, pulled those on, and took off down the hall.

Davis's home was a ranch. Three bedrooms and a bathroom off the long hallway that opened up to a living room to the left and the dining room to the right. Beyond the dining room was the huge kitchen, then a mudroom-slash-laundry room with a door that led to the garage. On the living room side, there was a small entryway with a closet and the front door. All the walls in his house were painted the color of mud which would've been bland if his couches weren't navy blue with mustard yellow toss pillows and two swivel chairs that were mustard yellow with a kickass cream and navy pattern. His dining room table was a large rectangle of recycled barnwood. Under a heavy layer of varnish the old peeling paint on the boards was still visible. The chairs around it were so dark blue they were almost black. And after the party when I helped Brooklyn and Sadie clear away all the decorations I found that Davis had multihued blue placemats that were kickass.

His house sat on a postage-stamp-sized lot with his back-yard taking up most of the square footage. Lush green grass, and he'd used rocks instead of mulch around the perimeter to the house. The only feature out back was a built-in barbecue and smoker. Between the two grills big pieces of slate created an area you could use to set utensils or serving dishes. I hadn't gotten the chance to ask last night if that outdoor kitchen area was already there when he bought the house or if he'd built it.

I was yanked out of my musings when I heard, "You do not come to my house and lay this shit on me."

That was Davis.

"No, let me rephrase, you don't come to my house for any reason ever."

That was Davis again.

"What's going on?" I asked.

My brother's angry gaze sliced to me, dropped to my bare legs, traveled up the length of me, and he narrowed his eyes.

"I see you're not wasting any time enjoying what fifty-large bought you," my brother said and turned his angry scowl back to Davis.

Bought you?

"Get the fuck out of my house."

"I need a word with my sister first."

"I already told you, that's not happening."

"Right, I see. Think because you bought pussy—"

"Careful, Zeus, that's my *wife* you're talking about."

"That's my sister I'm talking about, asshole."

My eyes were bouncing back and forth between the two men, trying to understand what was happening but getting more confused by the second.

"Jane ceased being your sister the moment you called her pussy. Now, you can get the fuck out of my house, or I can put you out, but you're leaving."

Trevor being the asshole he was crossed his arms over his chest and stared at Davis. I knew what this was. I'd seen this side of my brother from the time I'd understood what the word stubborn meant. He was settling in for the showdown. He wanted Davis to put him out. He wanted the confrontation, he got off on it. Sometimes I'd wondered if Trevor liked beating on people or if he liked to be beaten. Or if he was just too stubborn and stupid not to pick a fight with someone who could very obviously kick his ass. And it was obvious, between Davis and Trevor, Davis would wipe the floor with him and not just because Davis had a few inches on my brother. Trevor didn't take care of himself. He used intimidation and the threat of a whole MC coming out en masse to get people to do what he wanted.

"Just leave, Trevor," I waded in.

My brother's gaze swung back to me. His mouth twisted in an ugly way and he spat, "I don't give a fuck whose property you are, we gotta talk about Dad. We do that here or you come with me to the compound."

I was absolutely not going to the compound ever again.

"There's nothing to discuss."

"If you think that, you're stupider than I thought."

I heard Davis's menacing growl but ignored it.

"Then I'm stupid." I shrugged. "But Davis is right; I've ceased to be your sister though he's wrong about the timing. I stopped being that when you decided to one-up Dad. I've told you before and this will be the last time I say it, Trevor, so listen up. I'm dead to you."

"You weren't dead when your ass came to me needing help," he rightly reminded me. "I wasn't dead when I sent this motherfucker to get you safe. But now you're takin' his cock like a good little girl I'm suddenly dead to you? Fuck you, Rinny."

Shot. To. The. Heart.

Rinny.

God, I hadn't heard that since I was a little kid.

Trevor was the only person who called me that nickname.

"Trev—"

"Never thought I'd see the day," Trevor snarled. "My sister sellin' her pussy for protection."

My brother aimed that blow where he knew it would gut me. It landed so precisely I jerked back. But the wall of fury now rolling off of Davis was what had me taking a step back.

"You're done," Davis barked. "Always thought you were a motherfucking piece of shit but you standing here, spewing that bullshit just to hurt your sister is next-level asshole."

Trevor didn't spare me a glance as he spewed more venom.

"Wrong, Wright, this ain't done. It'll never be done. Like it or not your new snatch has my blood. You wanna keep her—"

Trevor didn't finish.

He couldn't, not with Davis's hand around his throat, pushing him back until Trevor's back hit the wall beside his front door.

"You even look at her funny, I'll end you," Davis stated, tone deceivingly calm. "You come near her, and I swear to fuck, my face will be the last thing you see before you quit breathing. Test that, motherfucker. I've been itching to put you down. Give me a reason and I'll have no problem scratching that itch."

Davis let go, opened the door, and waited.

Trevor looked over Davis's shoulders and locked eyes with me. In another life, my brother could've been more. He could've found the strength to fight his demons. We could've left together and been a family.

Tears pricked my eyes. I blinked to hold them back but

they escaped. Trevor watched them roll down my cheeks. His jaw clenched and pain filled his eyes—the only sign that somewhere deep maybe there was the tiniest shred of my brother left.

Without another word, Trevor walked out the door. Davis threw it shut with a mighty heave that damn near shook the house when it slammed. He locked it and turned on me.

"Jane—"

"What did he mean you bought me?"

Davis's whole body tensed.

"Don't listen to shit, baby, I didn't buy you."

"Then what does enjoying what fifty large bought you mean?"

"Jane, baby," he started and took a step in my direction.

I took a step back.

"Why won't you tell me what that means, Davis?"

"Fuck," he rasped and scrubbed his hands over his face.

My confusion turned to dread.

"Tell me what he meant," I demanded.

"It's not what you think."

That dread balled in my stomach. That was what someone said when it was exactly what you thought and they were going to make excuses for it.

"Then tell me, goddammit!" I shouted.

"Baby, let's—"

"Tell me, Davis, or I swear to God, I'll walk out of here and you'll never see me again."

Shit, why did I say that? I didn't mean it. I didn't want to walk out and never see him again.

Davis's expression darkened and he called my bluff. "There's the door." He swept his arm wide in the direction of the door.

Shit.

Shame crept in.

"Please tell me what—"

"Nope. No way are you getting away with that bullshit you just spewed."

I clamped my mouth shut. As it would seem I was infected with the same affliction Trevor had—stubborn and stupid.

"Davis—"

"Think before you say something you might not be able to take back," he warned. "Take a breath and think about me and the man you know I am. The work I do. And if that doesn't lead you to know *without question* I am not a man who would buy pussy and take payment for protection then we have a serious fucking problem."

Okay, I'd crossed a line threatening to leave.

That was stupid.

But his response to that was uncool.

Though a man he hated had just been in his house and I'm positive Davis hadn't invited him in, which meant Trevor had pushed his way in.

And on top of all of that my brother had called me "pussy" which Davis had made known he didn't like.

Yeah, I'd screwed up making that stupid threat.

It was time to pull up my big-girl panties and admit I was being dumb.

"That was a stupid thing to say, especially because I didn't mean it. On top of that I insulted you and I didn't mean to."

Yet again, Davis proved he was perfect and too good for me when he nodded.

"I didn't buy you, but I did pay your father off."

A chill ran up my arms, which contradicted the fire that was sparking in my veins.

"You paid him off?" I hissed.

"Actually, I paid your brother back. He paid off your father."

"You paid my brother back?"

"Yup. Didn't want that shit hanging over your head, you feeling like you owed him, when you absolutely don't. Also knew you hate knowing that Zeus used money he got from selling whores, drugs, and guns."

"Trevor bought me—"

"No, he did not. That right there is why I didn't want you to know. Your dad's a dick, Jane. He found out you were married to me, and just like we planned that made you off-limits. Your dad blamed Zeus and felt like making him pay. Until he just pulled this shit, I almost respected that gesture, your brother forking over fifty K and not bitching about that. Doing something for his sister. But, I couldn't let that stand because I don't trust the fucker. And also I'll repeat—I knew you'd hate knowing he made that payment with dirty money. So I paid him back. Obviously, he wasn't happy Wilson made the drop. Now I don't know if that's because he was trying to do something good for his sister and I fucked that play or if he was pissed because now he's got nothing to hang over you. What I do know is, I don't give the first fuck why that asshole is pissed. He can bitch and rant all he wants. What he's never going to do again is come in our home—*your* home—and disrespect you. Taking that a step further, he fucks with you in any way I'll make good on my promise and he'll find himself dead."

He was right, I didn't want my brother doing anything for me with dirty money and that included handing my father fifty-thousand dollars to buy my safety. And that was exactly what that pay-off was about. The whole reason my father wanted me was to pay off a debt and I'd bet he was into someone for fifty-K.

That was what I was worth.

Fifty thousand dollars.

"Dead?" I whispered.

"Dead," he confirmed.

"You'd kill Trevor?"

"If he fucks with you in any way I'll rip his throat out and do it with a smile on my face."

He was serious.

Davis would do that.

"I'm not sure——"

"I'm sure enough for both of us," he interrupted.

I closed my eyes, not sure what to think, but I knew what I felt. The problem was I was afraid what I was feeling made me just as bad as my brother and father.

"You're my wife," Davis rumbled. "Even if you weren't you're still mine."

My eyes snapped open and I took in the man in front of me. None of the anger had subsided though I knew it wasn't directed at me. I'd apologized, he'd accepted and moved on. It was that easy with him.

"I know you. The way you grew up, women were property," he continued. "So I feel the need to make sure you understand when I say you're mine, I don't——"

"I know what you mean," I cut him off.

I drew in a breath through my nose, gathered all the courage I could find, and gave him what he needed to move all the way on and end this conversation.

"Thank you."

Davis's eyelids slowly lowered and when they reopened the relief was stark.

That spoke to the heart of who he was.

He was nothing like my father or brother. He would resort to violence to protect me, not for greed or power.

"Do we need to talk about what your brother said?" he asked.

"Which part?"

"Any of it?"

I replayed the unpleasant conversation, or at least the parts I remembered, and decided I didn't want to talk about it.

"No."

"Don't bury that, baby. He said some fucked-up shit. You need to talk it out, I'm here to listen."

That was sweet.

"Hate to break this to you, but that was nothing. Actually, on a scale of one to Zeus he didn't even break a three with how ugly he can get."

Davis's brows drew together and his expression became ominous.

Mistake.

Big mistake.

"Honey, I'm used to it."

Ominous became dangerous.

Abort mission.

Shit.

"The only thing I need to talk about is the fact that I know the brother I once loved is gone. Logically I know this. I think even my heart knows he's not the big brother who had protected me. But sometimes, it's hard to wrap my head around hating him. I know I should. I know who he is. I'm not in denial or anything. But I just can't really hate him like I should."

"You shouldn't hate him."

I jerked back thinking I must've heard him incorrectly.

"What?"

"Baby, hate is an ugly burden."

"*You* hate him," I pointed out the obvious.

"Damn right I do."

Hm. That was interesting.

"So, it's okay for you to take that burden but not me?"

"Yes, Jane. I'll take that burden and carry the weight of it so you can live free and easy."

"You know you're giving me a complex, being so perfect," I blurted out. "I need you to do something like kick a cat." I slapped my hand over my mouth and shook my head. "I can't believe I just said that. I'm a hundred percent against animal cruelty. I don't even think raccoons should be trapped and relocated. It's not their fault we're taking over their habitat. They were here first. People should learn how to lock their trashcan lids, not disturb nature."

Oh, God, I was totally babbling.

Unfortunately I went on.

"I think this is what a mental break feels like. Do you think that's what this is? I'm jabbering on about raccoons and nature."

"Jane."

"I'm being serious, Davis, Trevor might've pushed me to a full-on come apart this time. He's insane. He pimps women. He's a drug dealer. He sells illegal guns."

"Baby."

"Yet you tell me not to hate him. That you'll hate him so I don't have to feel that burden."

"Jane."

"Why? Why would you do that for me?"

"Baby."

The weight of my brother's visit crashed over me. No, that wasn't what had my heart pounding in my chest and me wheezing to breathe.

"I was raised by club whores and a man called Satan," I panted. "No one has ever loved me."

Davis didn't let me finish before he prowled to me, captured my face with his hands, and growled, "Now someone does."

After he delivered that velvet blow he kissed me.

Not hard and deep.

Soft, slow, and thoroughly.

Until he made me a true believer.

Trevor had lied.

Real love existed.

It was just that he was a man too broken to give or receive it. And with that, I felt sorry for my brother. He'd never know this feeling. He'd never know how good it felt to give or receive love. He'd never know the sweet simplicity or how complex and overwhelming the emotion could be.

Oh, yeah, I felt bad for my brother because this felt…beautiful.

CHAPTER NINETEEN

It had taken some convincing after my meltdown to get Davis to drop me off at Smutties on his way to work, or to get him to go to work at all. While I was in the shower, which regrettably he hadn't joined me for, he'd called Wilson to tell him about my brother's visit. He'd also told him he was taking the day off. He was still on the phone with Letty explaining how we were both still jet-lagged and taking the day to lounge around and he'd drop me by the bookstore the next day.

He'd hung up, poured me a mug of coffee, and looked completely unrepentant about lying to Letty and changing my plans without asking.

After that I'd had my second meltdown, this one thankfully not as embarrassing nor emotionally charged so maybe I'd just ranted. Through this Davis listened, argued his position which was that he wanted me to rest and relax and get used to my new house. I ranted more, explaining that I wasn't going to bail on Letty the first time she'd invited me to her bookstore. He argued she understood. I explained how I didn't renege on my promises, and while I didn't make a pinky promise, I'd still given my word so I was going and I'd walk if I had to.

Davis gave in. With a harassed sigh, he left me to my coffee while he got dressed to leave.

Now I was standing in Smutties gawking at the twenty boxes of books that had been delivered that morning.

I wanted to tear into those boxes and see the beauty that hid inside.

A very pregnant Letty bent and looked as if she was getting ready to pick up a box that had a red sticker on the side that clearly stated it was HEAVY.

"What are you doing?" I snapped.

"Oh, God, not you, too."

"Not me, too, what?"

She straightened and held up the box cutter I hadn't seen.

"I can still open boxes. I'm fat, not—"

"You're not fat."

Letty sighed and shook her head.

"I'm totally fucking this up. I'm the fun one. I'm the crazy one. I'm supposed to be welcoming you to the sisterhood and here I am being a total grouch."

What was it with these people and their honesty?

Seriously, didn't they try to keep anything close to the chest?

"You're not being grouchy. I overstepped."

She stared at me, this time studying me until I wanted to squirm.

"You didn't overstep, Jane. You thought I was going to pick up the box. I'm being extra grouchy today because I have a thousand things I have to get done and I'm too tired to do them. River's riding my ass to slow down and I don't mean that as bitchy as it sounds. My husband loves me and worries, but still, I have a business I have to run but I can't do that huffing and puffing every five steps because I'm growing Bigfoot in here." She placed her hands on her belly and gently, reverently, rubbed up and down.

"This morning my brother showed up at Davis's house and it got ugly. He called me some bad names, Davis didn't like that too much, and told him if he even looked at me funny he'd put him down. After that I kinda had a nervous breakdown, told Davis he was too perfect, and to kick a cat."

"Kick a cat?" she breathed.

"Right? Totally psycho. Poor Davis. But it ended okay. I think he told me he loved me——"

"You think?"

I glanced around the kickass bookstore to make sure the three women who'd come in to browse were far enough away they couldn't hear.

"I told him I was raised by club whores and Satan. That's my father's club name and it totally fits. Anyway, I told him that no one has ever loved me and he said, now someone does. So, I think that was him telling me he loved me. Or I could just be going crazy, which at this point is totally possible." I paused for a breath and finished with, "Oh, and my father basically sold me for fifty thousand dollars, which Davis paid."

Letty's head jerked to the side making her long, black pony-tail whip her in the face.

She was completely unfazed by the hair whip.

"He sold you for fifty thousand?"

"Yup."

"What a dick."

"You got that right. So, you're stressed and pregnant and not at the top of your game." I shrugged. "I'm in the middle of a mental break and fake married. I think we should be BFFs."

Letty smiled wide before she busted out laughing.

"Sorry, Jane, Brooklyn's got the top BFF spot."

"Bummer."

And I meant that. Letty seemed cool.

"But a girl can never have too many sisters."

I wouldn't know. I'd never had a best friend or sisters.

"Right," I murmured and glanced down at the box.

"Jane?"

"Huh?"

"Babe, look at me, yeah?"

God, why was I so awkward?

I locked eyes with Letty. Nothing but warmth and under-standing shone.

"I mean that."

Before I could make more of an ass out of myself the door chime rang. I glanced over my shoulder to see Mia walking in.

I'd met her last night and her fiancé Cole. The woman was very pretty but there was a confidence about her that made her stand out. She'd also been overly apologetic about lying to me about Wilson. It wasn't her fault I'd run. I could've told the truth when she'd asked if I was in danger. It was water under the bridge as far as I was concerned but when her eyes came to me they were guarded. So maybe it wasn't or maybe she was having second thoughts about welcoming me into the group.

"How grouchy are you today?" she asked as she approached.

Letty flipped her off.

"That grouchy."

"Awesome," she said then looked over at me. "Hey, new friend, want to go get a cup of coffee with me?"

Wait.

Was she talking to me?

Was I the new friend?

Were we friends?

"Don't freak her out. She's had a bad morning. Her dickwad brother showed up, got Davis all riled up, he told her he loved her but didn't say the words outright but he so totally loves his fake wife and she found out her dad sold her for fifty grand."

"Whoa. That's not a bad morning, that's a dumpster fire. All the more reason to get coffee."

Just to say, Letty's warning about not freaking me out was belated; therefore, it was too late. I was freaking out.

It only got worse when Letty slammed her hands on her hips and very irately griped, "Why are you trying to steal Jane for coffee?"

"I'm not trying to steal her."

"Liar," Letty straight out accused. "You're stealing her."

"Fine. I am. You have Brook. Sadie and Sloane are thick as thieves. I get Jane. I'm new, she's new, and I want her."

What? Mia was new? What did that mean? Last night all the women were super close. I'd have bet they'd all been friends since childhood.

For the second time that day I found my head bopping back and forth watching a verbal tennis match.

With one last glance between the two of them I butted in, "I'm in serious need of coffee. I will love you forever if you bring me a large black but I think we should stay here and help Letty unpack these boxes."

Mia gave Letty a triumphant smile.

"Sure thing. I'll be back. Letty, tall decaf, extra caramel or is it a vanilla week?"

"Hazelnut," she hmphed. "And if Sadie has any cinnamon rolls left I'll take two of those."

Mia was completely unperturbed by Letty's snappy answer. She smiled and turned to leave.

"Wait, I need to give you money," I called out to Mia.

"My treat. You can grab the next one."

I was ridiculously happy at the thought of there being a next time.

I turned back to Letty and asked, "Where should I start?"

"You don't have to unpack books. We can sit and chat. I promise as soon as I get a cinnamon roll in me I'll be fine."

"Letty, I'm unemployed now. You have me all day or until Davis gets done with work and comes back to pick me up. Put me to work."

Letty's head tipped to the side and she smiled.

"Unemployed?"

"Well, yeah, I quit my job to go on the run."

"You're hired."

"Hired?"

"Yup. You start today. Mrs. Simpson works half days, Mondays, Wednesdays, and Fridays. But she can't be here alone. I have another part-timer, Laurie. She's super cool and only works when her kids are in preschool. She's in Tuesdays and Thursdays. And I just hired Patty—she's in on the weekends only. We're only eight to six except on the weekends and we stay open from eight to eight, but like I said, Patty has that covered. So your hours would be eight to six Monday through Friday, cool?"

Cool?

Letty was offering me a job.

All she knew about me was my brother was the president of an MC, a criminal, and someone her police officer husband was trying to take down, and I was fake married to a friend of hers.

That was it.

Oh, and she knew I went to elementary school with Sadie.

"Yeah, cool."

The chime went off and Mia came back holding a tray of coffees and a white paper bag.

"That was quick," I noted.

"Sadie knows better than to keep a-ready-to-pop Letty waiting. What'd I miss?"

"Jane's working at Smutties. Today's her first day," Letty happily chirped.

Mia looked from Letty to me then back to Letty and when she did her eyes got squinty.

"I knew I should've taken her with me."

I wasn't sure exactly what was happening but I knew it felt good.

It felt real.

It felt almost as beautiful as waking up next to Davis.

Almost…

CHAPTER TWENTY

If River didn't sit his ass down I was going to duct tape him to a chair.

"Has he been like this the whole time I've been away or does something have him extra tweaked today?" I asked the room at large.

Cole chuckled from his place across the table from me. Sitting next to Cole, Rhode snickered but didn't look up from his laptop. Jack didn't make a sound but he smiled and pretended to be reading whatever report he had on the table in front of him.

"You're not tweaked?" River inquired.

"No, I'm pissed as fuck, brother, but I'm not trying to wear a hole in the carpet. Sit your ass down, you're freaking me out."

River turned his icy blue eyes on me and squinted.

"I've got a pregnant wife who will not, no matter how many times I beg her, take time off of work. She's due any week now and she's acting like she has months. On top of that, I've got a cop who sits at a desk in an office next door to mine who's a fucking prick and getting cagier and cagier by the day.

We've got a dead seventeen-year-old who took her own life because she was used to blackmail cops. As you know, Blake and Johnson are cooperating. They handed over the pictures but they're not in possession of the recording." River's lip curled in disgust. "Zeus ambushed Blake while he was getting gas and showed him the recording. He caught Johnson coming out of the grocery store. But still, both men were mailed the pictures. Since Phillips isn't talking we can only assume something similar happened to him. But now I'm wondering, how deep is Phillips? Blake and Johnson couldn't get that shit off their conscience fast enough when they were approached. Both men admitted they were fucked up and didn't know how to get out from under this without going down as a pedophile. Age of consent in Idaho is eighteen. Even if it was younger seeing as both men are cops, therefore in positions of power, they'd be charged. They knew this and couldn't find an out for a stupid fuckup but an innocent one. Now with all that, I think I'll stand and pace."

Now I felt bad I opened my mouth.

I didn't touch on the topic of Letty. The woman thought she was superwoman, though she loved River and was so over-the-top happy to become a mom I knew she'd never do anything to jeopardize the baby.

"How deep is Phillips?" I asked.

"Don't know but my gut says Zeus has something else over him."

"He's married. The other two aren't."

"Thought about that, but still something's not right. IA gave him an out. Pending the investigation if termination is the outcome, which in a way is fucked but they're gonna be fired. Bottom line is, Sommer Levine was underage. But if the investigation goes their way the records will be sealed. They won't get a letter of recommendation but it won't be public record why they were let go. So, Phillips could lie to his wife about why he was fired and she'd never know."

"Or she could push him to file for wrongful termination," Cole put in. "They have a new baby at home."

"Or Sommer wasn't the only girl Zeus supplied to Phillips. Or he's been giving Zeus information. Or he's been covering for Zeus giving him safe passage. Whatever it is, something is not right with that asshole. I can feel it. Blake and Johnson are torn up. Full of remorse. Almost sick with it. Phillips? He's walking around whistling Dixie like he's living high on life."

I turned to Wilson who was at his normal seat at the head of the table.

"What do you think?"

"I don't know the man like River and Brasco do. Though Brasco thinks he's an asshole and wants his ass canned, he thinks he's not cooperating because of the wife and kid."

"And he might be right," River conceded. "I could be way off base with this but my gut says there's more."

If River felt something was off, I believed him. But there was feeling something and then there was being able to prove it.

"Butch agreed to a meet," Rhode announced. "Thirty minutes. Riverstone Park."

Riverstone was twenty minutes away with no traffic. It was spring in Coeur d'Alene which meant there'd be traffic.

"And he wants Davis at the meet," Rhode went on.

This wasn't surprising. I'd married Zeus's sister; no doubt he wanted to know what was going on.

"How much does Butch know about Jane and me?"

"Everything," Wilson said then amended. "Or I should say, everything up to the wedding. He's not in the know that you've fallen for your fake wife. Which I didn't get to tell you last night, is impressive. I figured it'd take at least six months before you got her to thaw."

"Life's too short to fuck around," I returned.

"Ain't that the truth?" River muttered.

"Says the man who waited fourteen years to make his move," I quipped.

"Yet, here we are, my ring on her finger and my kid planted in her belly. How long did that take me?"

To the best of my recollection Letty was pregnant within a few months of River moving to Idaho and he snuck her off to get married shortly thereafter. He might've waited fourteen years but when he decided to stake his claim the man moved across the country and did that in record time.

Still, I had him beat.

I'd fallen for Jane almost instantly. Fought that attraction for less than a day. Circumstances were such she had to marry me to get safe. But a smart man knows when to press his advantage. She was my wife and I had no intentions on letting her go.

"You know you fucked me with that," Rhode piped up. "And then Reese did when he married Sadie. Now Davis. My woman's unhappy we've been engaged for freaking ever and we're still not married."

"So take a personal day, take your woman and son, and go get hitched," Wilson reasoned. He stood. "But you need to wait until Davis and I get back from our meet. I need you to get into Stone Phillips' computer, phone, cloud service, all of it. If you need help call Shep."

"It goes without saying I didn't hear anything about hacking a police officer's devices. Though, if I were you I'd check out the wife, too."

"Got it," Rhode muttered and went to work.

Forty minutes later Wilson and I were walking the path around the man-made lake making our way to the amphitheater.

"Jane okay after what happened this morning?" Wilson asked.

"She says she is."

"But you don't believe her?"

"She said that this morning wasn't as ugly as she's gotten from her brother. That I believe. She wants to hate him but she can't. She remembers the boy who protected her when she needed him. She can and does separate the two. But, no, I don't believe she's okay after the shit her brother said. No sister can be okay with that. Fuck, Wilson, the asshole called her pussy right to her face. She didn't even flinch."

"Love's a strong emotion. It drives us to do all sorts of fucked-up shit. It can be the most beautiful thing in the world or it can slice you to shreds and make you wish you were dead. I get how she'd struggle with that." Wilson paused and blew out a breath. "Don't let that shit fester in her. She's gotta get it out."

"Got any bright ideas how I can get her to stop loving a fucked-up piece of shit?"

"Love her harder than the memory of the boy who protected her."

"Come again?"

"Love her *harder*," Wilson slowly drawled. "Once she knows the feel of a healthy, genuine love, she'll understand what she feels for her brother isn't love and it never was. It's a memory. You can love a memory but not love the person attached to the memory. That's what she needs. That's what will get her through."

Fuck, if he wasn't right.

"Thanks."

"Anytime."

Butch came into view. The man looked worn down and ragged.

"Christ," I mumbled under my breath.

"He wants out," Wilson said. "He's had enough of this shit. I wouldn't be surprised if he asks to be pulled."

If Butch quit, the DEA's case would fall apart. It would take years to get someone patched into the MC and in a place of knowledge. Butch was the DEA's only shot at taking Zeus down.

"I heard congratulations are in order."

Not the lead-in I'd expected from the man but still, I dipped my chin.

"Got something for us?" Wilson cut to it.

I watched the muscle in Butch's cheek jump—a clear sign the guy was agitated. I hadn't known him long, but I'd never seen him show any emotion. I knew Wilson saw it, too, when he frowned and uncharacteristically used a tone that was reserved for the women who were part of the family.

"*Brother.*"

Butch cleared his expression, looked me dead in the eye, and got down to business.

"Zeus is pissed as fuck. Last few days all he's done is rant about you. Wilson delivered that money and the dumbfuck twisted that as disrespect."

I couldn't stop my smile.

"I see you think that's amusing, but trust me, nothing that asshole does can be categorized as anything but what it is— jacked up, fucked up, and stupid. Word's flying he has a sister, something he'd managed to keep under wraps all these years. Which proves he's a dumbfuck, with all his ranting about how you paid for snatch and how that pussy belonged to him, he's now exposed her."

I clenched my jaw. I didn't like hearing that shit firsthand out of Zeus's mouth and I didn't like hearing it secondhand. But I had bigger problems than some jackass calling my woman 'snatch'.

"I got Jane covered," I told Butch.

"Yeah, heard about that, too. Even though Zeus was in the know and played a part now he's bitching how you've claimed her. At first I thought he was playing the part, towing the line so word would hit the street and make it back to Satan. Now I'm not so sure. I think he thought, this being fake, either you'd get shot of her when it was over or she'd dump you. After this morning I think he now understands his sister is no longer his in any way she could've been."

"It's good he understands that, Butch. She's mine. I'm keeping her. I told him this morning and I'll tell you, he pulls that shit again or harms her in any way you won't have to quit because you'll be out of a job when I put Zeus to ground."

"Maybe you can make my year and do that soon."

"Working on that," Wilson told him.

Butch fell silent and seemed to be struggling with something.

Wilson and I patiently waited for a man who was at the end of his rope work out what he needed to work out.

"I can't see my way through this," Butch rasped. "The longer I'm under the less I can get clean. I go home at night and still the stench lingers. I need the fuck out. That has to happen soon. So my dilemma is, do I go all-in with Takeback and fuck the DEA's case or do I suck it up, find the fortitude to see this through, and take down Zeus and his supplier?"

"You gotta do what is right for you," Wilson immediately answered.

"Yeah, and if his supplier's a cartel out of Mexico that's on the rise and getting to the top at an alarming rate, what then? Does your advice change?"

"You've got to do what's right for you," Wilson answered again.

Butch blew out a breath and ran a hand through his greasy hair. He didn't hide the disgust when he wiped his hand on his dirty jeans.

I'd only ever known this version of Butch. I wondered what he was like in his daily life before he grew his hair long, stopped washing it, and maintained an unkempt beard.

He looked the part of an outlaw.

But it didn't fit.

He looked like he was coming out of his skin.

"I'm digging around for those recordings and pictures."

"We need an admission," Wilson told Butch.

"Working on that, too."

Fuck yeah. If Butch could get a confession that would move this shit along.

"Last thing and this is just talk right now, he's talking about selling off the girls. He's bitching it's too much hassle keeping a stable of whores. Though the way he takes freebies, not sure he'll actually do it since he likes to get laid and he can't find a woman in a thirty-mile radius to give him head since he's such a twat, much less fuck him, I'd bet he doesn't actually sell."

If there was an award for King of the Douches Zeus would hands-down win.

"Whatever you need we're here," Wilson offered.

Butch gave Wilson a chin lift and started to turn when Wilson went on. "Anything you need, whenever you need it, no questions you call any of us."

"Appreciate that, Wilson."

With that he walked away.

"We've got to step this shit up. Brasco's ready to explode. River's a loose cannon. And that man needs to get the fuck out before he suffocates."

Wilson was not wrong.

CHAPTER TWENTY-ONE

"I can't believe you have the new Elizabella Baker *Blackguard Security*." Mia snatched the book off the sorting table and stared at the cover. "I've been waiting for this since you gave me *Reclaiming What's Mine*. I've been dying for Maddox's book."

Letty grabbed the paperback away from Mia and held it to her chest.

"Well, you're gonna have to wait a few more days. I had to beg Elizabella to send this to me early."

Obviously I must've looked lost because Mia went on to explain, "Okay, so, Elizabella writes kickass romantic suspense. You know, hot, growly alpha guys but with really great plots. In book one there's this hacker, right?" She paused so I nodded. "The hacker's name is Maddox. Now this hacker is the bomb, can find anything. *He's* there in the background doing *his* thing. Only communication is done electronically." I wasn't sure why Mia put such an emphasis on "he" and "his" but when she paused I nodded again. "Well, get this, it turns out, Maddox isn't a *he* she's a *her*. Not only that, she's this badass rocker chick with purple hair and the mouth of a sailor. And in that book

Letty's selfishly keeping to herself is her story. I hope she runs Chance ragged before he calms her ass down."

I kind of hoped this Maddox gave Chance a run for his money, too.

"Jane reads historicals and fantasy," Letty announced.

I startled and turned my gaze to Letty.

"I can't believe you remembered that."

"Don't be too impressed. I can't remember the titles or authors you've bought just the genres. You also filled out the questionnaire at the check-out counter when I was polling my customers on genre and trope."

That was ages ago.

"Well, I'm impressed," I told her and went back to sorting books. "And when you're done with Elizabella, I want her after Mia. I need some badass, purple-haired hacker in my life."

"*Oh*, an RS virgin," Mia singsonged. "You need to read the *Guardian Defenders* series." She stopped to pin me with a stare I didn't understand. "The *real* Guardians by the one and only Kris Michaels. Then when you're done there move to Susan Stoker's OG SEAL books. After that you move to anything Olivia Michaels, Anna Blakely, Abbie Zanders, Caitlyn O'Leary and if you want hot male-male action, Annabella Stone for the win. If not, Bella Stone, plus she's hilarious. When you finish those you'll be ready for Elizabella Baker."

"I think maybe you should write those down?" I suggested.

"Write what down?" Davis asked.

I glanced to the front door then back to him.

"How'd you get in here? I didn't hear the door chime."

He dangled a set of keys from his index fingers.

"From the back. Got the keys to the castle."

"We were just giving Jane book suggestions." Mia winked. "You're welcome."

"Please tell me you included some Lexi or Willow in there," he returned.

"Lexi Blake is Cole's favorite romance author," Mia explained. "It's BDSM."

I swear I felt my cheeks heat.

"Don't worry," Letty cut in. "We'll work you up to bondage, butt plugs, and spanking."

Butt plugs?

Holy shit.

"Two things," Letty continued but this time looking at Davis. "The Brittney Sahin you ordered came in. It's by the register."

"I forgot to add Brittney to the list. Read her, too," Mia whispered.

"And two, Jane started work today."

Davis's eyes cut to mine.

"Say again?"

"Jane's working at Smutties."

I watched as a slow, beautiful smile tugged at Davis's lips.

"Excellent."

I hadn't given much thought to what Davis's reaction would be to me starting a job but his huge smile and saying 'excellent' like he was genuinely pleased for me came as a surprise.

"We'll head over to Wolf Lodge to celebrate."

"Celebrate?"

"Baby, you started a new job. We're celebrating at Wolf Lodge unless you don't like—"

"I love Wolf Lodge."

"Then steaks it is. Are you done or do you need me to come back and pick you up?"

Oh, shit.

Right, I didn't have a car anymore. I'd sold mine to fund my escape and put extra money in the bank to keep current on my rent.

"I don't have a car," I muttered.

"So?"

"So? How am I going to get to work? How did I forget?"

Oh, no. I felt another freakout happening.

"Jane—"

"How did I forget, Davis? That's important. And my stuff. My rent. I have a—"

My rant was cut short when Davis hooked me around the waist and pulled me close. When he had me where he wanted me, his hand went to the side of my neck and he gave me a gentle squeeze.

"Calm down."

I wasn't sure I could calm down now that my mind was whirling.

"I can drive you to and from work until we get a car situated for you."

We?

I didn't touch that.

"I can't ask—"

Another squeeze.

"You didn't. I offered."

"Patty!" Letty weirdly shouted. "Your place is furnished, right?"

"Uh, yeah."

"She's twenty, totally responsible, going to NIC, and working here is her second job. Last weekend I heard her bitching about her roommate bringing home guys when she's trying to study and is looking for a place. Want me to ask her if she's interested in your place?"

Whoa.

Giving up my place was a big step.

"Might not hurt to ask if she's interested," Davis softly murmured.

As mentioned, my mind was whirling, so I blamed my

heart sinking at Davis's noncommittal on the fact that I wasn't thinking straight.

Did he not want me to give up my place?

Was he planning on me moving back into it soon?

"It's not like you'll be using it, but until we can arrange for the rest of your stuff to be brought over…" he trailed off and his eyes roamed my face. "Babe?"

"The rest of my stuff?"

"I thought we talked about this this morning."

I didn't need to cast my mind back to this morning to know we absolutely didn't discuss me moving my furniture.

"No, we didn't."

"I told you I liked waking up to you."

I waited for him to say more. When it was apparent he wouldn't, I asked, "Is that bad-boy code for you're moving your furniture into my house?"

Davis's lips twitched and Mia laughed, but it was Letty who spoke.

"Maybe when we were unpacking books this afternoon I should've warned you about a few things."

I turned my head to look at her.

"Such as?"

"Once they move you in they don't let you leave. Or if they move in with you they don't leave."

That would've been a helpful conversation.

"And they're bossy," Mia put in. "Don't forget to tell her about that."

"They're bossy," Letty repeated as if I hadn't heard Mia.

"I figured out the bossy part on my own," I noted.

Davis's hand slid up into my hair and he gently brought my attention back to him.

"As amusing as this is, maybe we can get back to what you're going to do with your place."

This was not a decision one made on the fly. A decision such as this needed careful thought and consideration. Maybe a glass of wine and pen and paper to make a list of pros and cons. A good amount of thinking had to go into something like this. I didn't want to be known as the floozy who moved in with a guy after…

I didn't finish that thought.

My mind was no longer whirling. I was stuck on a singular thought—*I didn't want to be known as…*

My whole life I'd weighed my actions. I'd always been careful, never wanting anyone to think I was like my father, then later my brother. I'd kept my thoughts to myself, I'd stayed hidden, I'd washed myself down to the point I had nothing.

All because I cared what other people thought, even though I lied and said I didn't.

I was cruising in my forties and I'd had two lovers.

Two.

That was insane.

Totally bonkers.

All because I was afraid people would look at me and think, *Yep, she turned out to be a biker whore.*

As if a woman getting herself some made her a whore, yet when a man did it he was a stud.

That was a whole 'nother conundrum for a day when I wasn't freaking out about a variety of traumas that had hit and I wasn't wrapping my head around the fact I'd screwed up my life. Okay, maybe I hadn't screwed it up but I'd wasted it.

It was time I started doing what I wanted, when I wanted, and how I wanted to do it.

Did I like waking up next to Davis? Yes.

Was it too soon to give up my place and take the leap of actually moving in and not just staying there to keep up the fake marriage? Did I give a crap?

"Call Patty and see if she's interested. I have seven months left on my lease."

As soon as the words came out of my mouth Davis smiled.

No, that wasn't right. His face lit and his beautiful eyes got soft. He openly liked my answer and I liked knowing he gave that to me.

Then I went on. "I have money in the bank to cover my rent. If Patty takes over and I don't have to pay my rent I can use that to buy a car. But in the meantime if you could take me to and from I'd appreciate it."

"Absolutely."

"I can pitch in, if the guys get busy," Mia offered. "I leave the office at six so you'd have to wait a few minutes."

My new friend would help.

I had a friend.

Actually I had three—Davis, Mia, and Letty. And if I was lucky I'd get to know the others and they'd be my friends, too.

"Thanks, Mia. That's cool of you to offer."

"Don't mention it."

"I *love* this!" Letty excitedly bounced.

"Damn, woman, stop moving like that before that baby makes an early appearance," Davis groused.

Letty stopped bouncing. The excitement slid from her face and she gave Davis a dirty look.

"Why is it that men think babies just slide out of our vaginas?" After she asked that she rocked my world. "Maybe that's why you want fifteen kids. You think all Jane has to do is dance a little jig and they'll just fall out."

Hold on just a second…fifteen kids?

Eek.

I was not having fifteen kids.

"Seven," Davis weirdly said.

"Seven, what?" I inquired even though I was afraid I knew the answer.

"Kids."

"Seven?"

"Yup."

"And who do you plan on birthing your seven children?"

Davis smiled, confirming my fears.

But still, my belly warmed he thought I'd be the mother of his children.

"I'm not having seven kids."

"Three," he countered, "and I'm firm on that. Though if they're all girls we're going for another one in the hopes that it's a boy."

I could do three. Four would be a stretch but I had a feeling Davis wanting seven kids meant he planned on being a very hands-on dad, so I wouldn't be alone in wrangling our brood.

Was I seriously negotiating how many children we were going to have?

Yep.

And I gave no shits what anyone but him thought about it.

"If the first three are all boys, we're going for another in hopes of having a girl," I said.

"Works for me since I want a baby girl."

Good Lord, I think my womb just contracted.

"Well, I'm glad that's settled," Letty announced like she'd orchestrated that whole conversation for her amusement. "I'll call Patty when I get home tonight and text Davis her answer. Now, get. Go enjoy your celebration." Letty added an eyebrow wiggle and a smile.

I didn't have a phone so she'd text Davis.

As strange as it was, I didn't mind not having a cell phone. Actually, I liked it. No time suck, mindlessly scrolling social media, no notifications. I was present in the moment without the distractions.

And finally I had a life to be present in.

I WAS NAKED, draped across Davis's chest. His hand was stroking down my back, my belly was full of really great food, I'd had two orgasms, Davis had had one. We were both mellow, lying in bed, coasting off to sleep.

So I didn't know why I brought it up but I needed to get it off my chest.

"I'll pay you back the fifty thousand."

Davis went solid underneath me.

"It'll take a while but I will."

His hand stopped stroking and I should've taken that as a warning but I kept going.

"I only have about ten thousand left in my savings account, maybe a little less. Now that I have a job and if I'm not using it to pay rent I can get myself a car. I get the feeling Letty just needs me to help at the store while she has the baby. When she lets me go I'll find something else. I'll need to pay it back in installments. It's gonna take time, but I'll pay it all back."

Davis remained statue-still and tense. The only movement coming from him was the rise and fall of his chest which was now visibly noticeable.

"Davis?"

"Give me a minute."

Seeing as the tone of his voice was abrasive and rough I'd give him five. I started to roll away.

Davis locked me in place so I made the wise decision not to struggle.

He didn't take a minute. He also didn't take a breath before he irately rumbled, "How much do you think your safety's worth to me?"

Oh, boy.

"That's not the point," I braved.

"Fifty large? A hundred? A million? The way I see it I got off easy."

We were cruising into dangerous territory.

Dangerous for my heart.

Dangerous for my peace of mind.

Just plain dangerous.

"Davis," I whispered.

"I should give you this, but I'm not. But I'm gonna take the time to untwist this so it doesn't fester. I didn't buy you. You're not my property. You're not indebted to me."

"Can you see how I might think I am?"

"Yes."

Okay, this was good. He could see it my way.

Unfortunately he continued, "I can see how you grew up with those two assholes how you'd think that. I can see you growing up and them not showing you how *priceless* you are, how you'd think that. I can totally see you growing up not feeling the love of your father, your family, how you'd miss it. So here you go, Jane; I didn't have a father but I had a mother who loved me and showed it. She worked her ass off to give me what she could. Every holiday, every birthday she'd spend her last dollar making sure I knew she'd give me anything in her power."

That was sweet. I was glad he had that from his mother. I loved knowing that about him, but I didn't understand why he was sharing it right now.

Suddenly he rolled me to my back. Davis shifted, planted his elbow on the mattress while his other hand came up and he brushed my hair off my face.

"You're worth it," he said, his voice no longer a rumble. Softer, full of something huge. Just hearing it made my stomach knot.

"Davis—"

"You're worth it, baby. Every dollar. Every penny."

I felt tears gather.

My stomach clenched tighter.

"Davis—"

"Do you honestly think I'm going to find this smart, stubborn, sweet, beautiful woman and not do anything—any-fucking-*thing*—to keep her safe? It's money, baby. It comes, it goes, you earn it, spend it, blow it on stupid shit. A couple grand on a TV for no reason other than it's time to upgrade, a thousand on a phone, ten bucks a day on coffee—meaningless, stupid shit that all adds up. So when you think about it, Jane, fifty thousand so you can breathe easy and be safe is nothing. I had it but even if I didn't, mark this—I would've begged, borrowed, and knocked off a bank if I had to."

I stared up at Davis's handsome face. His blue eyes holding mine—open, out there, completely vulnerable.

Pure Davis.

"I don't know what to do with this," I whispered.

"Do with what?"

"This. You. Feeling like this. Making friends. Falling for you. Learning what love truly is. Being happy and scared at the same time."

And that was to only name a few of the whats I didn't know how to process.

"Just go with it."

I felt a smile tug at my cheeks, but it never fully formed.

I wasn't complaining.

It was difficult to smile through one of Davis's mind-bending kisses.

And I'd take one of those any day of the week.

CHAPTER TWENTY-TWO

"The guy's an asshole but I think River's wrong," Cole said from beside me.

From my place in the driver's seat I watched Stone Phillips make his way across the parking lot of the rundown apartment building toward his car.

"That was quick," I noted.

"He's always quick," Cole returned.

Cole wasn't wrong. The last three days we'd been following Phillips he got in, got off, and got out. The getting off part being with one of Zeus's girls, not his wife.

We sat quietly and waited for Phillips to drive off.

"Hope to fuck this one talks," Cole clipped.

The last two women hadn't. They'd flatly denied that Stone Phillips had paid them a visit.

We were out of the car and nearly to the steps that would lead us to the second-floor apartment Phillips had just exited when Cole said, "Cool of Jane to go full-time at Smutties. I know River's grateful. Means starting next week Letty's down to only a few hours a day."

I knew River was grateful. He'd stopped into the office the

day after Jane took the job. Relief was written all over the man's face but still he expressed his gratitude.

"She only has a few weeks left before the baby's here. It'll be good for her to relax."

"Yeah, no doubt."

"NOT SURE IF you were right about Phillips being in deeper than we thought but he's providing services," Cole announced as soon as we hit the conference room and he saw River standing inside the room with Brasco next to him. Wilson, Rhode, Asher, and Reese sat around the table.

Needless to say the hooker talked. It had taken some coaxing but she wanted out from under Zeus and once we'd convinced her we could help her disappear she unloaded.

"What'd you get?" Brasco asked.

"Tensions are high between Zeus and Phillips," I started. "Zeus wants more protection for his routes—those being him bringing drugs down from Canada. Phillips is getting antsy. He knows IA's sniffing around, putting on the pressure. He wants Zeus to cool his shipments."

"How'd you get this?"

"Cara Bristol, club name Sparkle," Cole spat.

"How does a biker bunny know this?"

Cole smiled though he couldn't hide his disgust.

"She's a favorite of both Zeus and Phillips. On more than one occasion when they were done with her, thinking she was passed out, the dumbfucks talked. The woman might be a hooker but she's not dumb. She went home and wrote that shit down in her diary."

Cole tossed the leatherbound book on the table.

"Dates, what was said, any names mentioned," he finished.

"Jesus," Rhode ground out and reached for the book. "Seriously?"

"Seriously," I confirmed.

"Why'd he visit her today?" Brasco asked while moving to stand behind Rhode.

"To get his weekly blowjob," Cole sneered and continued. "Last weekend Phillips was at the compound. She said that he and Zeus got into it worse than normal. Phillips refused a job, Zeus reminded Phillips if he didn't do the job, his wife would get a visit and see the video. Cara didn't know what video Zeus was talking about but she saw Phillips get in Zeus's face." Cole paused, shook his head, and continued, "The moron threatened to kill Zeus if his wife saw that video."

"What'd Zeus say to that?" Wilson quizzed.

"He laughed. Phillips didn't find it funny and left."

"We might have a problem," I rejoined. "Cara says that Phillips was agitated today. She's friends with the other two we talked to, probably the reason she didn't look all that surprised when we showed up. The other two warned we'd paid them a visit, but both of them told Cara he was rougher than normal and pissed off."

"You think Phillips is planning on taking out Zeus?" Brasco didn't sound all that torn up about the prospect of that happening.

"That'd solve a lot of problems," Reese muttered.

He wasn't wrong. It'd put Zeus down permanently and Phillips in the joint where he belonged.

I felt no remorse thinking this about my wife's brother. The world would be a far better place without Zeus in it.

"Where's Cara now?"

Cole turned his attention to our boss and told him the bad news.

"At a safehouse waiting on you to make some calls to get her out of Idaho."

"Fuck, seriously?"

"Yep. The woman wants out. She'll testify to what's in that book as long as she gets a new identity. Oh, and she's requested a beach."

Wilson made an angry sound that had River chuckling.

What a difference three days and your wife hiring an employee makes. The man no longer looked like he wanted to rip someone's head off.

"Want me to make a few calls?" Brasco offered.

"No, but thanks. I'll call my man in Nebraska, have him come pick her up."

Guess Cara Bristol wasn't getting a beach.

But she was getting out and if she stayed the course she'd be free to make something good of her life.

"Are you going to talk to Jane about this?" Rhode's question wasn't an accusation, he was just curious.

"Fuck no. She has a new job she loves, a new home she's getting comfortable in, she's sorting out Patty and when she's moving in, she's enjoying getting to know the girls, and for the first time in her life has friends, and she's shopping for cars online. No reason to bring that asshole into our lives."

"If Phillips takes him out…" Rhode let that hang.

"Then he does the world a favor." I shrugged. "I'll deal with any emotional fallout if Phillips manages to off Zeus. But Jane mourned the loss of her brother a long time ago. Trevor holds a place in her heart; he saved her from being violated by a man from her father's club. Trevor got a beat down from the club for his efforts. That's when he turned. I don't understand it, I don't want to understand it, but for that single act of protection, he has my gratitude. Now, Zeus, he can rot in hell and take his fucked-up dad with him."

"Are you shitting me?" Wilson growled.

"Nope. He used to sleep next to her so no one would come into her room in the middle of the night. He stopped her from being raped. So, somewhere deep, *deep* down, buried under all his bullshit he's got at least an ounce of good in him and I'm grateful he used it to protect her."

The men around shifted uncomfortably.

A reminder that even the evilest of men can have a moment of decency.

Trevor Lawrence was a piece of shit. I despised him, but I still had to acknowledge the good he'd done.

"Well, fuck me," Rhode grunted.

That about summed it up.

I WALKED IN THE HOUSE, smelled something cooking, and smiled.

When our meeting with River and Brasco ran late, Mia offered to pick up Jane. Actually, offer was a stretch. Mia had come into the conference room and announced she'd called Jane to tell her she was picking her up and waved goodbye.

I'd excused myself to call Jane at work to make sure she was okay with this. What I got was a happy, chatty Jane telling me about her day and how excited she was to spend time with Mia. Selfishly, I wanted her to want to wait for me. But hearing the enthusiasm in her voice soothed a worry I didn't know I had.

Jane was happy.

She fit in, she was getting close to the women.

And she was excited about something.

I went back to the meeting smiling, uncaring the guys were giving me shit when I rushed through the rest of the brief.

Now I was walking into the house I shared with my wife who was right then in the kitchen with the house phone pressed between her shoulder and her ear and she was bobbing her head up and down while dumping steaming water into the sink.

I leaned against the doorjamb and listened.

Jane barely spared me a glance but she did give me a big, bright smile before she went back to concentrating on what she was doing.

"Yeah, rearrange whatever you want. And I'm sure Davis and I can move it in here or we'll get rid of it."

Davis and I.

Fuck yeah, Jane was settling in.

"Perfect. I'm so happy you like it." Pause. "Great. Call me if you need anything." Another pause. "Sure thing. Bye."

Jane finished pouring the water into the sink. Chunks of potatoes came next, then she set the pan into the other side, and took the phone from her shoulder.

"That was Patty," she chirped.

Jane was chirping excitedly.

Fuck, yeah, she was settling.

"She wanted to know if she could rearrange the living room. Of course I said yes. She had her own bedroom furniture so she doesn't need mine."

"If you like your bedroom furniture we'll replace mine."

Beautiful green eyes gentled.

"Your master furniture is nicer than mine. But mine's nicer than what you have in your spare."

"Then we'll change out the spare. Is Patty good to wait until the weekend or does she need me to round up the guys and do it tomorrow?"

Jane's eyes moved over my shoulder.

"Right. I'll call Cole and Asher and get them to go over there tomorrow after work and move it."

"Really?"

She still didn't get it.

But if she did, I wouldn't be able to remind her, and I seriously liked Jane's response to my reminders.

I pushed away from the door frame, hooked her around her waist, and hauled her close. When my lips were on hers I muttered, "Yeah, baby, really."

I felt her grin against my lips, then I kissed my wife.

CHAPTER TWENTY-THREE

I was changing out the books on the new release table, half listening to Mrs. Simpson on the phone while wondering if Letty would fire me if I took the advanced reader copy Harloe Rae book. Surely she wouldn't have time to read it with an infant at home. Even if at four weeks she was bragging about him sleeping through the night.

My body gave an involuntary shake thinking about Letty and baby Maverick. One could say Letty was very vocal about the pain she was in. And after she'd gotten the epidural she was very descriptive in her account of the pain she *had* been in and vowed she was scheduling a c-section if there was to be a second child.

I'd thought she'd gotten off lucky when her labor had only lasted three hours. But when we'd been allowed to go into her room and in her arms was a nine-pound ten-ounce adorable baby boy, I thought a c-section was a good idea for the next Kent baby.

The only not so great part about Maverick's birth was River's siblings, Echo, Phoenix, and Shiloh weren't there. Letty went into labor two weeks early, which I thought was a blessing because that nine-pound ten-ounce adorable baby boy could've turned into ten-pounds ten-ounces. And we'd all heard enough from Letty waxing poetic about her vagina not being equipped to have Kent babies. A ten-pounder might've ended in Mav being an only child.

Hell, the experience was enough for me to tell Davis we weren't having kids—ever.

But then the next week when Letty and River started having visitors and Davis and I went over to see the baby, I'd quickly changed my mind, and secretly I hoped I'd have a nine-pound baby with chubby cheeks and fat rolls. He was beautiful with Letty's dark hair and River's icy blue eyes. And seeing River cradle his son made me want to take my husband home and tell him I was done with the pill and wanted to get down to business.

Fortunately logic won out.

I wanted more time with just me and him.

"Jane, when you're done, Letty sent new pictures," Mrs. Simpson called from her chair behind the register.

The books could wait, I needed my daily Maverick fix.

When I got close the scent of Chanel N°5 filled the air and I smiled.

Mrs. Simpson was pure class. Dressed to the nines, full face of makeup, and expensive perfume to come to work in a bookstore. I'd fallen in love with her instantly. She was kind and wise and gave the guys ruff as often as she could, which was every time one of them came into the store.

"Isn't he a doll?" she breathed and shoved her phone out for me to see.

I took Mrs. Simpson's phone and stared at chubby-faced Mav puckering his cute little baby lips.

"Absolutely."

I handed Mrs. Simpson back her phone.

"When are you and Davis going to have children?"

I was used to this. Mrs. Simpson might've been class but she was nosey with a love for a good conspiracy theory. In the last four weeks she was positive the garbage collector was a Canadian spy, the neighbor above her who had moved into Letty's old apartment had ties to the mob, and she was certain the wildlife management had released cougars on Tubbs Hill to keep the bear population down. The woman was a riot. I adored every minute I worked with her.

"Not for a while," I answered as I walked back to finish the new display.

"Don't wait too long, dear."

When she didn't continue and I knew she had more to say I looked over to find her staring off into space.

"Mrs. Simpson?"

"When you're in the thick of it, it's hard. There will be days when your home is a mess, dinner will be burnt, you'll want to cry in exhaustion or scream in frustration. But every minute is worth it. Every second a gift. Then they grow up and that happens too quickly. Your home is back in order, no more toys scattered about, no more piles of laundry, no more dinners to burn. And you miss it. You miss the noise and runny noses and the bickering. But then it starts over and your grandchildren come over and you have to put all the breakables up and get baby gates so they don't fall down the stairs and you get to bask in the beauty you created." Mrs. Simpson's eyes cleared and she smiled sweetly. "You and Davis get to break the cycle. You two will create a beautiful family. You will love your children—not more than other parents do, but perhaps differently because you and Davis, you know and you learned, and you overcame. Don't wait too long, Jane. All that beauty awaits."

I felt tears prick the back of my eyes. But before the first one could fall, Mrs. Simpson abruptly changed the topic.

"My granddaughter, Atlee, will be coming to visit soon. That was her on the phone. She called to tell me about her promotion.

She works in Las Vegas. I wish she'd picked another city without as much crime but she's in the hotel industry so Viva Las Vegas it is."

It took me a moment to get my emotions under control and wrap my head around the subject change.

"That's cool. I can't wait to meet her."

"No, Jane, that is not *cool*," she replied haughtily "My granddaughter's upcoming visit is magnificent. It is one of the many ways *I* get to bask in the beautiful family *I* created."

I couldn't help my lips from twitching. But I held it together —barely. Knowing that if Mrs. Simpson saw she'd launch into a twenty-minute lecture about how my generation has butchered the English language.

Thankfully the chime over the door went off so I had an excuse to smile.

I turned to welcome the newcomer but stopped when a uniformed police officer frowned at me.

"Hi, may I help you?"

His frown turned into a look of distress but it seemed off.

"Are you Jane Morgan Wright?"

"Yes."

"Is your brother Trevor Lawrence?"

My blood ran cold.

What had my asshole brother done now and why was I being bothered at work?

I straightened my shoulders, unwilling to allow anything my brother had done to make me look like I was anything but the respectable, honest citizen I was.

"Yes," I answered curtly. "However, I would appreciate—"

"I'm sorry, ma'am, but Trevor's been in an accident. He's critical."

My stomach hollowed like I'd been punched in the gut.

"What?"

"You're his next of kin. It's not looking…good."

Oh my God.

"It's not looking good?" I repeated.

"I'm here to escort you to the hospital."

I stood frozen, not believing what I was hearing.

It wasn't good.

I could read between the lines.

He wasn't going to make it.

Suddenly all I could picture was my big brother standing next to me on my first day of school. He'd squeezed my hand and sent me off to class. My brother getting me medicine when I was sick because my father couldn't be bothered. Trevor making me canned soup and grilled cheeses for dinner because that was all he knew how to make.

"Go, Jane. I'll call Davis and tell him to meet you there."

"Um?" I stammered.

Did I want to see Trevor before he died?

I wasn't sure.

Maybe I should wait for Davis to take me.

"Miss, you don't have long."

Davis worked thirty minutes away. He was closer to the hospital than I was. He could meet me there.

God, why did I argue with Davis when he took me to look at cars? He wanted me in an all-wheel drive. I wanted a Honda like I'd sold before I went on the run. We bickered, I got stubborn, and now we were going out again this weekend to look. I should've gotten the Subaru.

"Miss?"

Why was I thinking about cars when my brother was in the hospital dying?

"Yeah, I'm coming. Kootenai Health, right?"

"Yes," the officer pushed out.

I turned to Mrs. Simpson.

"You'll—"

"Go, darlin'. I'll call Davis." She already had her phone in her hand.

Davis would meet me there, then I'd decide what I wanted to do.

I followed the police officer out to the street. A black Ford Explorer was double-parked. He helped me into the front seat, jogged around the hood, and got in.

We were at the end of the block at the stop sign when I got my shit together enough to speak.

"I didn't ask your name."

Out of the corner of my eye I saw him move in a flash.

Then pain exploded at my left temple.

So much pain it was a relief when everything went black.

I WOKE UP TO SHOUTING.

I was no longer in the car. My head throbbed and the cop yelling was not helping the pain. I reached up to rub my temple and that was when the reality of my situation came crashing down around me.

My hands were cuffed in front of me. My ankles were definitely secured to the chair I was sitting on and I didn't have to look to know there was something around my chest. I leaned forward and the strap didn't budge.

Oh, shit.

Holy shit.

I glanced around a room I'd never been in and couldn't find a single object that would give me a hint as to where I was.

"I told you, motherfucker, you gave that recording to my wife I was going to kill you. The bitch took my kid and left. Now you pay."

That didn't sound good.

There was silence but not for long when the cop turned to me and smirked.

"Yeah, Zeus, you're gonna pay or your pretty little sister—" The cop went silent.

Zeus.

Of course my brother was involved.

I wasn't surprised but I was shocked.

And the shocking part was how I'd gone from being scared my brother was going to die while I was standing in the bookstore to now wanting to kill him myself.

"I already have the bitch," he continued. "Now, you bring me my money or she bites it. Choice is yours but you better make it fast. The old broad already called Wright."

Mrs. Simpson.

Davis.

Panic crept in.

Was Mrs. Simpson in danger?

And Davis, he was going to go crazy—like tear-the-city-apart crazy looking for me. He'd go to Zeus first. He'd go to the compound and go up against all of the Horsemen to get to my brother.

"No bullshit, Zeus. You come alone with my money or she's dead. You got twenty minutes before I'm gone."

Twenty minutes.

Then I was dead.

CHAPTER TWENTY-FOUR

Wilson and I walked out of the police station in silence.

That morning Stone Phillips had turned in his badge and gun and told his captain he was quitting effective immediately. After a month of nothing. No more visits to whores, no runs for Zeus, nothing. The man went to work, went home to his wife. It was like he'd had a complete about-face. IA was scrambling. Brasco was on edge. River had looked like he wanted to put his fist through a wall and that was putting it mildly.

"What'd we miss?" Wilson muttered when we hit the parking lot.

"Yo!" Brasco yelled from behind us and both of us turned in unison to see him jogging out the door. "River just got a call from Letty."

Cold started to infuse my spine.

Letty calling River wouldn't cause Brasco to run out and get us unless something was wrong with Letty or Maverick.

"Letty okay?" Wilson asked, thinking the same as me.

Brasco shook his head.

"Mrs. S called her when she couldn't get ahold of you."

"Me?" I asked. "Jane need me?"

I reached into my pocket and pulled out my phone. I'd silenced it before our sit down.

Eleven missed calls.

Ten from Mrs. S, one from Letty.

No texts.

That cold turned arctic.

"Davis," Brasco started. "Come back inside a minute."

I felt Wilson get close knowing that if Brasco wanted me back inside whatever he had to say wasn't going to be good.

I ignored Brasco and pressed Mrs. S's contact.

"Davis," she answered.

"What's—"

"Jane's brother has been in an accident. I've been trying to call you to tell you."

Fuck.

"I'm on my way."

I was lowering my phone when I heard Mrs. S yell.

"Repeat that, Mrs. S?"

"She's not here. She went to the hospital with a police officer."

The ice in my veins crystalized.

"She left with a police officer? Did he give a name?"

"No, just that it didn't look good for her brother. I told her to go and I'd call you. He was taking her to Kootenai Health. They left about ten minutes ago. Meet her there."

I disconnected without a goodbye and looked at Brasco.

"Do you have any reports of Zeus being in an accident?"

"No, but I wouldn't. River's calling the hospital now."

"Mrs. S said that Jane left with a police—"

"We're checking on that, too."

He was checking on that.

Fuck.

I turned to Wilson who had his phone up to his ear.

"Do we have anyone on Phillips?"

Wilson shook his head but held up his hand when he started talking.

"You called," Wilson spoke into his phone.

With each second that ticked, Wilson's shoulders got tenser and tenser. And seeing that, my gut started to roil.

"Right. Good. Send us your location and we'll follow you."

Wilson lowered his phone and angrily stabbed at the screen.

"What the fuck—"

"Cole, I'll be sending you a location. I need you and Asher to kit up and roll out. Send Reese to Smutties to sit with Mrs. S. Armed and alert. Rhode stays at the office with Mia. Tell Jack to go to the compound. Do not approach, just wait for my call. Out."

Wilson turned to me and ripped the Band-Aid off. "That was Butch. Zeus just tore through the common room of the compound, yelling on the phone. He went to his office, came back with a big black duffle. Butch says that's where his safe is. He also heard Zeus say, 'If you touch my sister I'll kill you.' After that he ran outside, jumped on his bike, and hauled ass."

"I'm gonna kill them both," I seethed.

"Good news for us is, Butch has a tracking device on Zeus's bike. Butch is on his bike following Zeus, and he's shared his location with me. We're following."

"Hold up and I'll—"

"No," I cut off Brasco.

"Davis—"

"You can stand here and piss me off or you can turn around and let me leave so I can go get my woman."

It took a moment, one that felt like for-fucking-ever. I knew the reason Brasco paused was because he was a good man, a good cop, and he knew if he turned his back that was him letting me loose on Zeus and Phillips. A good man would struggle with this, the knowledge that I was going to commit a felony then later deny it. My team would cover for me, Shep would be called in to help with the cover-up. Brasco knew it and he'd be put in a position to have to come clean and rat me out or live with knowing I killed two men and not say anything.

Brasco turned his back.

Then he flat-out ran back into the building.

"Giving us a head start," Wilson mumbled. "Let's go."

We were in the company SUV rolling out of the parking lot when Wilson tossed me his phone.

"You navigate."

I went to the Find Me app, tapped on people and only saw one name: UNKNOWN with a location in Hayden.

"Make a right. Stay on Government Way."

I focused on the dot slowly moving on the map and watched the phone shake in my hand.

"Hold it together."

I clenched my jaw to stop myself from lashing out at Wilson and kept my attention on the dot.

"He turned onto Honeysuckle." I glanced up at the traffic in front of us then looked back at the map. "Next light, turn right."

"Davis—"

"It'll take forever sitting in this traffic. Turn right on Hanley, it's all residential."

"Brother, I don't give a fuck how we get there, but you need to breathe."

I was breathing.

"I am."

"You're jittery as fuck. Breathe. You need to be on point when we get there, not vibrating."

Wilson made the turn, the traffic subsided, and we were finally moving faster than a snail's fucking pace.

"At the roundabout you're exiting on 4th."

If the first three are all boys, we're going for another in hopes of having a girl.

I heard Jane's soft voice come at me.

After Mav was born she'd changed her mind.

Seven might work.

She'd said that while lying naked on top of me after we'd visited Letty, River, and Mav the first time.

We're back to only three, with the option of the fourth. Babies are a lot of work.

She'd told me that when I'd gone to Smutties to pick her up after work and Letty had spent a few hours in the store with the baby.

And finally…

Last night with her on her side, me behind her with my arm around her holding her close.

Thank you, honey.

For what?

For giving me this.

She was finally settled, her and the girls were tight, she'd made my house our home. We butted heads, we bickered, we made love, we laughed, she smiled all the time.

Finally.

She got it.

All of it.

And Zeus's bullshit had to go and fuck her up again.

Oh, yeah, I was going to kill him.

This was going to end for him.

"Where to?" Wilson pulled me from my thoughts.

Shit.

I looked around then back at the map.

"Stay on 4th until you hit Honeysuckle, stay right."

I zoomed in on the map.

"Butch is stopped. It's a residential neighborhood right before the beach."

I thought about the one and only time I'd gone to Honeysuckle Beach. I'd taken my mom there when she was visiting. Nice houses, close together like in my neighborhood.

Wilson's phone rang in my hand.

I didn't bother asking him if I should answer. Unknown caller meant it was Butch.

"How far out are you?" he asked as soon as I answered.

"Maybe two minutes. Do you have a house number?"

"The situation has deteriorated. You better make it one."

I was struggling to get oxygen into my lungs.

"House number?"

"You'll see the bikes."

With that he hung up.

"He says we have a minute."

"We'll—"

I felt my chest vibrate.

Wilson didn't finish.

But thank fuck he sped up.

The SUV wasn't even at a full stop when I jumped out and ran.

Neither Zeus nor Butch bothered to hide their bikes. Phillips' black Ford Explorer was parked next to a detached garage.

When I got close I heard Phillips' angry voice shouting.

The first gunshot rang out and I pushed harder. The second shot went off and fear ripped through me so violently I stumbled.

I got to the door, opened it, and without care or concern for anything but getting to Jane I ran into the garage.

The sight before me sent bile rushing up my throat, choking me.

Jesus fucking shit.

Jane was on her back in a tipped over chair, Zeus haphazardly on top of her, blood covering his back. But it was Jane's wide-open eyes that held my attention.

"Go." Wilson shoved me out of his way and I went to Jane.

"Close your eyes, baby," I whispered.

"Get him off of me."

Her voice was clogged with emotion.

I wanted this done for her but I didn't want her to see any more than she had.

"First, close your eyes."

"I already saw. I saw everything."

Fuck it.

My hand went to Zeus's neck. I felt for a pulse, found none, and it was only by a miracle I was able to contain my urge not to toss him off of Jane like the piece of garbage he was.

Once I had Jane free, I noticed the angry red swelling on the left side of her head.

Whatever control I had was slipping.

"He's dead, too," she said.

"Who?"

"The cop who took me. He's dead, Davis. Just please untie me."

She'd seen them both die.

I made fast work of cutting the zip ties off her ankles and then cut the rope that held her to the chair. The handcuffs would have to wait until I found a key.

"I'm gonna lift you up."

Jane nodded.

I reached down, scooped her up, and as soon as I had her in my arms she shoved her face into my neck, and it was then she let out an unholy wail.

"I got you, Jane."

From head to toe she shook.

"I got you, baby."

Without a word I walked out of the garage.

Jane sobbed.

"You're safe."

I heard sirens in the distance and I knew Jane did, too, because she went stiff in my arms.

"Jane?"

"He's a cop."

"He was a dirty cop who your brother was blackmailing."

"You knew?"

My steps faltered.

"I knew," I confirmed.

I opened the back of the SUV and maneuvered into the back seat without letting go of Jane.

"As soon as I can get a key I'll uncuff you."

Jane nodded but didn't speak.

Zeus was dead.

The gratification I thought I'd feel was absent.

The anger, the fear, the knot in my gut, all gone.

Jane was in my arms and breathing.

"Love you, baby."

"I love you, Davis."

I closed my eyes and savored the feel of her words.

"Everything's gonna be okay."

"I know, Davis."

"I'm gonna make sure you're okay."

"I know, honey."

WILSON AND COLE were still in my living room sitting on the couch when I came back from laying Jane down. The sun had come up and both men looked like shit.

"Thanks, but you—"

"You good?" Cole asked.

Fuck no, I wasn't good.

I'd sat next to Jane at the hospital while she had to relive the whole fucking nightmare—from being taken from Smutties, punched in the car, coming to and hearing Phillips threaten Zeus, to being gagged while she waited for her brother to arrive. Then I had to watch her break down when she got to the part about how Zeus died. And that fucker was still fucking her over even in death. He'd taken the bullet meant for Jane. Stepped right in front of it and took one to the heart. It was a damn lucky shot seeing as Butch opening the door startled Phillips so his shot went to the side—just enough to catch Zeus while he ran at his sister like some superhero jumping on top of her to protect her.

Butch had turned on Phillips and shot him.

The rest I knew because I was there.

The rest being nothing since Zeus and Phillips were both dead and I didn't get to take out either one.

"I'm good," I lied.

Wilson tipped his head and studied me.

"Tell me, Davis, what part are you more pissed at; Phillips taking out Zeus, Butch taking out Phillips, or that the villain in this story died a good guy?"

All of that and more.

I ground my molars together.

"Be grateful. The two times she needed him, he stepped up. Let her have that. Give her that piece of her brother."

My jaw started to ache.

"And get her to talk to Letty. She knows a thing or two about complicated siblings."

Fuck. I hadn't thought about that.

"Take tomorrow but I'd like for you to make the meet with Butch before he leaves."

Butch needed to get out of Idaho before his cover was completely blown and the Horsemen found out he was undercover DEA.

"I'll be there."

Wilson took a breath and when he exhaled I braced.

"No doubt he was a piece of trash," Wilson said softly. "But he emptied that safe and went to her. It wasn't enough, but he tried."

Wilson spoke the truth. Zeus had shown up about twenty grand short of what Phillips wanted. I wasn't feeling like giving him a pass on this. The jumping in front of a bullet and dying for his sister, I was grateful for that.

Him rushing out of the compound like a fucking outlaw asshole, no.

"He should've called me. I would've gotten the money and he knew it. He was being his normal stubborn, jackass, blowhard self. But, he's dead, so I have no one to get pissed at. It's a wasted emotion and I'd rather stop thinking about him and go take care of my wife."

It was a polite hint to leave.

One they both took without offense.

I locked up the house, didn't bother making coffee for the morning because I had no plans of letting Jane out of bed until dinnertime.

She'd been checked over at the hospital—no concussion, but she did have a nice-sized goose egg and some bruising.

So, yeah, she was sleeping all day tomorrow.

My head had barely made it to my pillow before Jane turned and cuddled into me.

"Thank you, honey."

I closed my eyes and breathed deep.

"Baby, I didn't do—"

"Yes, Davis, you do. Every day you make me feel loved. Every day you teach me how to love myself. Every day you make me happy. I know I'm going to be okay because you're sleeping next to me and I know you like it because you tell me you do. You're open and honest and too damn perfect but that makes me feel safe. I know you'll never lie to me."

"You never have to thank me for loving you."

"Well, I just did." She snuggled in. "So just go with it."

On a day as shitty as the one we'd had, I could not believe I was ending it roaring with laughter and Jane giggling in my arms.

Once again Wilson was right.

I had no choice but to be grateful.

CHAPTER TWENTY-FIVE

Three months later…

I watched Remington in his little boy tux weave through the crush of people on the dance floor until he made it out of the crowd and over to the remains of the decimated cake.

"Ten bucks says he just sticks his hand in and…"

Letty didn't finish.

Remy scooped up a fist full of his mom and dad's wedding cake and shoved it into his mouth.

"Your parents are never going to get that boy to sleep tonight after all the sugar he's eaten."

Mia wasn't wrong. Letty's parents were going to have one hell of a time getting that boy to sleep tonight when they took him home so Brooklyn and Rhode could spend the night alone up in their cabin.

"Aww, he deserves all the cake he can eat," Sloane put in. "He stood next to his dad through the whole ceremony and didn't make a peep."

This was true. Remy stood tall and proud next to his parents while they exchanged their vows. Now, Maverick on the other hand fussed at the end so I reached over to the pew in front of me. I took him from Tally and went outside so she didn't have to miss the service.

By the end of the twenty minutes I held him, my arms were burning. That boy had some heft to him and he squirmed around a lot.

"I'm getting a drink, anyone want anything?" Sadie asked the table.

"Girl, how are you going to carry all our drinks back by yourself?" Sloane asked and stood with Sadie.

"I'll go with and help," Mia announced. "Lets? Jane?"

"Water," Letty pouted.

She was still breastfeeding and had already had a glass of wine with dinner.

"Water, too, please."

Letty's head whipped to the side so quickly I almost jumped out of my chair.

"Are you pregnant?" she whisper-shouted.

"Jeez, calm down."

She comically widened her eyes and leaned closer.

"Well, are you?"

"No. I'm just thirsty."

She looked disappointed. I glanced at Sadie who shrugged. Next, I looked at Sloane who was smiling. Then to Mia.

"Now that she has one she wants everyone to have one," Mia explained.

"I do not."

"Yeah, you do. Last week you told me not to worry that vaginas shrink back," Sloane contradicted.

"You know, it's kinda strange this vagina kick you're on."

"Sloane brought up vaginas, not me."

Asher sauntered up. "Is Letty trying to talk you into getting knocked up again?"

I'd been around these men for months and there were times I was still taken back by how good-looking they were.

Letty rolled her eyes before they came back to me.

"Are you really sure you're good to stay on full time?" she asked.

"For the fifth time tonight, yes. I love Smutties. I never want to work anywhere else."

My sweet friend was killing me.

"Lets, it's been three months. I've told you I'm fine. I didn't need the week off you gave me but I appreciate it. Everything's good."

"The nightmares are gone?"

I glanced around the room and spotted Davis, Wilson, Rhode, and Brooklyn talking with Michael.

Tally was sitting at a table with Mrs. Simpson and a few older women I didn't know.

Remy was still running around dodging guests. I had no idea who a lot of them were, but Letty had said they were family friends. River was holding Mav, standing by the bar talking to his partner Brasco.

Cole, Jack, and Reese were sitting at a table laughing.

I was surrounded by good, clean people who had welcomed me into the crew and made me family.

It was no secret I'd had nightmares after Trevor died. I didn't hide it from Davis nor our friends. Each of the men had offered to listen if I needed to let the heavy stuff from that day go. The women had all circled around me like mama bears.

Mrs. Simpson had been right that day I was taken.

Davis and I were breaking the cycle.

We didn't need kids to do that.

We loved openly and honestly.

My husband had taught me how to do that.

When I was done taking in the room, I went back to Letty to answer.

"No. Not for two weeks."

"Good. And you're still talking to Dr. Shasta?"

Dr. Shasta was a sweet older woman who I'd spoken to twice a week for the first month. Then we moved to once a week. Now I was talking to her every two weeks and I'd probably do that for a while.

Something else this group taught me. Vulnerability doesn't mean you're weak. When it's given to the right person or people it strengthens your soul.

I am me.

Unapologetically me.

Jane Wright.

"Yep. It might take a while to work out my daddy issues."

"Daddy issues?" Davis asked from behind me.

"Yeah, honey. When your daddy's the king of the underworld you grow up with issues."

I heard Davis grunt before he kissed my head.

"Dance with me, wife."

It wasn't an invitation, it was a demand.

"Boss," I mumbled under my breath.

Letty's lips twitched before she gave me a full-on beautiful smile.

"I'll bring her back when I'm done with her."

"Take your time. I need to go find Mav. My boobs—"

"Nope. I keep telling you I don't want to hear about your boobs," Davis interrupted.

"Since when is everyone so touchy about boobs?" she pushed.

"Woman—"

"They're boobs. I feed my boy with them. Well, and sometimes River takes—"

"Make her stop." Davis whirled me around and demanded, like I could make Letty do anything when she was razzing one of the guys.

"Honey, you know if she wants to tell you about River sampling her—"

The rest of my statement was cut off.

Not by words but by deed.

Davis's lips pressed hard against mine. When he was confident I wasn't going to talk about Letty's boobs he pulled back and moved his lips to my ear.

"That shit just earned payback," he growled, and I shivered. "I see you like the idea. We'll see how much you like it when I keep you on edge all night and don't let you come."

Davis would totally do that.

"I promise I'll be good the rest of the night."

He slipped his arm around my shoulders and led me to the dance floor, turned me, wrapped me close, and started to sway.

"Do you want to get married?"

"Um, we are married."

"But do you want this?" He jerked his head to indicate the room.

I looked around again at all the smiling, happy faces, eating, drinking, dancing, communing, and having a great time celebrating Rhode and Brook.

"No. Do you?"

"Are you sure?"

"Honey, what's this about? Do *you* want this?"

That was the first I'd ever seen Davis look unsure.

"Dav—"

"I don't want this. But I'm not a woman and women tend to like this kind of thing. So if you want a real wedding—"

"A *real* wedding?" I cut him off. "Honey, I don't regret how we did it. It's us. It's ours. Every promise I made to you was real and I know damn well the vows you said to me were real. Everything might have started out backward but that doesn't mean it wasn't very right. So no, I don't want to remarry you."

"Yeah, baby, it is very, *very* right."

Surprisingly, my husband didn't kiss me, which was his way when I said something he liked. Instead, he held me close and swayed with me to a song I didn't hear a single word of.

I was too busy thanking my lucky stars, staring into my very real husband's beautiful eyes.

CHAPTER TWENTY-SIX

Wilson McCray

3 months later - Coeur d'Alene hotel bar

I threw back the rest of my whiskey and looked across the low round table to the two men across from me. I waited for the Japanese blend to work its magic.

No such luck.

The burn was still present.

"Have you spoken to Jack?" I asked Saint "Pete" Young.

"Respect, Wilson, you know I wouldn't do that shit."

He wouldn't. That was why he was taking time having this meet when he should've been visiting with his sister Mia the night before her wedding.

But that didn't mean he wouldn't poach one of my men.

"We have a situation in Honduras." Pete paused to look over at former DEA Agent Beckett Yates. Now clean-shaven, fresh haircut, and in a suit. Beckett looked nothing like Butch though he hadn't yet lost the wariness. After years undercover, I figured that would take a while. "Beck will be joining us in San Diego, but I need Jack. He knows the Eastern Caribbean Lowlands better than anyone I know."

This was true. Jack had spent a lot of his military career in Central America.

I didn't want to lose Jack.

But I was going to lose him all the same.

Fuck.

"My team won't be happy," I noted.

Pete set his empty glass on the table and leaned forward. His eyes glinted with unleashed anger.

"Your team will give their blessing when we lay out the mission," he countered. "Every thirty-six hours a woman dies in La Lima. Femicide isn't on the rise, it's at the peak. The time to step up was years ago when the gangs took over. Now it's way past time and I'm making it my mission to end the terror. Women are no longer safe to be alone in their own homes. They can't walk to the store, they can't work, they can't be out with friends without the risk of dying. This has to end."

The man wasn't wrong—it was time to put an end to femicide and Jack would be all over this operation and he'd have my team's blessing.

"Whatever you need from Takeback," I conceded.

Pete sat back and relaxed.

"Right now all I need is Jack but in the future we might need backup."

"Then you'll have it."

"Appreciated. Hate to cut this short but I need to get back to Mia and find Cole so I can threaten to kick his ass again if he fucks over my sister."

There was no chance Cole would fuck over Mia, he'd waited decades to have her again. However it was a brother's duty to threaten the man who was marrying his baby sister.

"And Beck needs to get back to San Diego before someone sees him. Though not many Horsemen are still around after the takedown and I'm not sure the ones who aren't behind bars are observant enough to recognize him now that he's lost the dirty biker look."

Dirty biker look was an understatement. By the end of Butch's time undercover he'd looked beat down and disheveled. As for the Horsemen, I wasn't giving any of those assholes any more of my time. Zeus dying put an end to the DEA's investigation. The members who Brasco and DEA had evidence on were locked up, the rest—and there were only a handful not caught up in the sweep—scrambled.

The Horsemen were no more.

Thank fuck.

"How's sunny CA treating you?" I asked Beck.

"Breathing clean."

Two words that said it all.

"Pleased for you." I turned back to Pete. "Don't get into a bust-up with Cole. It'd suck if you had a fat lip and a black eye in your sister's wedding pictures."

Saint "Pete" Young smiled. It was the kind of smile a man had when he knew his sister had found a good man who would make it his mission to make her happy.

"Yeah, that'd suck. See you tomorrow."

I sat back in the plush chair in the corner of the bar and watched the men make their exit.

Fuck, I was losing Jack.

Now that the Horsemen were down and Brasco and River weren't on edge it was time for Takeback to get back to work.

I shot off a text to my contact at Homeland to let him know we were available.

Before I could pocket my phone it buzzed in my hand.

Good timing. Two weeks. Las Vegas.

Las Vegas had earned its nickname honestly, there was no shortage of sin.

I sent a return text confirming we were in and stood to leave when a beautiful woman at the bar caught my attention.

Brunette, pretty face, full lips, curvy in all the right places, long legs, and alone.

Just my type.

I made a detour to the bar, left a stool between us, and sat down.

The bartender made his approach just as the woman turned to look at me.

Now that I was close I could see her big brown eyes were better than those long legs. And I was a sucker for tall women. My wife had been blonde, blue-eyed, and short. In the years she'd been gone I hadn't touched a blonde or a woman who didn't have some height.

"Another Hibiki?" the bartender asked.

"That and whatever she's having."

"Boulevardier. Makers," the woman smoothly put in. "And thank you."

The bartender made his leave and I went back to the woman.

"I'm Wilson."

"Atlee."

Unusual name.

"Fitting."

"What is?"

"Your name."

Those brown eyes lit with humor.

"Is this where you give me some cheesy pick-up line?"

Her smile was alluring, but her wit was what had me ensnared.

"I don't do cheesy pick-up lines."

"Are there *non*-cheesy pick-up lines?"

Oh, yeah, I was enthralled.

"Not that I know of."

Our drinks were placed in front of us, I picked up mine, motioned for her to do the same, and offered a toast.

"To a night full of orgasms."

She smiled wider and asked, "Would those be yours or mine?"

"Depends on what your plans are for tonight."

Our glasses were still close but untouched when Atlee volleyed, "I hope we're not toasting to a night of self-love. That would be disappointing."

Totally dug this woman.

"Finish your drink, Atlee."

I clinked mine against hers.

She took a healthy swallow.

I was losing Jack.

But that was a tomorrow problem.

Tonight, I had Atlee.

TAKEBACK CONTINUES WITH **DANGEROUS AFFAIR**... WILSON and Atlee's story.

I wonder what Mrs. S is going to think about Wilson and her granddaughter…;)

Don't forget to sign up for my **Rebels Newsletter** so you don't miss out on sales, freebies, up coming releases, and all things Riley.

ALSO BY RILEY EDWARDS

Riley Edwards

www.RileyEdwardsRomance.com

Takeback

Dangerous Love

Dangerous Rescue

Dangerous Games

Dangerous Encounter

Dangerous Mind

Dangerous Hearts

Dangerous Affairs

Gemini Group

Nixon's Promise

Jameson's Salvation

Weston's Treasure

Alec's Dream

Chasin's Surrender

Holden's Resurrection

Jonny's Redemption

Red Team - Susan Stoker Universe

Nightstalker

Protecting Olivia

Redeeming Violet

Recovering Ivy

Rescuing Erin

The Gold Team - Susan Stoker Universe

Brooks

Thaddeus

Kyle

Maximus

Declan

Blue Team - Susan Stoker Universe

Owen

Gabe

Myles

Kevin

Cooper

Garrett

Silver Team

Theo

The 707 Freedom Series

Free

Freeing Jasper

Finally Free

Freedom

The Next Generation (707 spinoff)

Saving Meadow

Chasing Honor

Finding Mercy

Claiming Tuesday

Adoring Delaney

Keeping Quinn

Taking Liberty

Triple Canopy

Damaged

Flawed

Imperfect

Tarnished

Tainted

Conquered

Shattered

Fractured

The Collective

Unbroken

Trust

Standalones

Romancing Rayne

Falling for the Delta Co-written with Susan Stoker

AUDIO

Are you an Audio Fan?

Check out Riley's titles in Audio on Audible and iTunes

Gemini Group

Narrated by: Joe Arden and Erin Mallon

Red Team

Narrated by: Jason Clarke and Carly Robins

Gold Team

Narrated by: Lee Samuels and Maxine Mitchell

The 707 Series

Narrated by: Troy Duran and C. J. Bloom

The Next Generation

Narrated by: Troy Duran and Devon Grace

Triple Canopy

Narrated by: Mackenzie Cartwright and Connor Crais

More audio coming soon!

BE A REBEL

Riley Edwards is a USA Today and WSJ bestselling author, wife, and military mom. Riley was born and raised in Los Angeles but now resides on the east coast with her fantastic husband and children.

Riley writes heart-stopping romance with sexy alpha heroes and even stronger heroines. Riley's favorite genres to write are romantic suspense and military romance.

Don't forget to sign up for Riley's newsletter and never miss another release, sale, or exclusive bonus material.

Rebels Newsletter

Facebook Fan Group

www.rileyedwardsromance.com

facebook.com/Novelist.Riley.Edwards

instagram.com/rileyedwardsromance

bookbub.com/authors/riley-edwards

amazon.com/author/rileyedwards

Made in United States
North Haven, CT
11 January 2024